MATT SHAW

and

MICHAEL BRAY

Matt Shaw / Michael Bray

A CIP catalogue record for this book is available from the British Library

ISBN 10: 1497364361

ISBN-13: 9781497364363

Art

Definition of art (n)

art

[aart]

1. creation of beautiful things: the creation of beautiful or thought-provoking works, e.g. in painting, music, or writing

2. beautiful objects: beautiful or thought-provoking works produced through creative activity

3. branch of art: a branch or category of art, especially one of the visual arts

P R O L O G U E

A new hotel. At least 'new' in the sense I'd not been there before. The hotel had existed on the outskirts of the town for a few years now. Not unpleasant but hardly like the pictures in the brochure. Old age and hundreds of guests hadn't been kind to it. Patches of stains on the walls; the dressing table by the long wall-mounted mirror chipped here and there; pages torn from the Bible I found in the top drawer of the bedside cabinet, for what purpose I'll never know; lime scale on the sink's taps in the bathroom; a discoloured rubber mat next to the bath - also complete with taps coated in lime scale. Clearly the cleaners haven't heard of the concept of elbow grease. Back in the main room and the bed sheets have seen better days. Had it not been for what was planned, I'd have asked for management to come by and change them. By tomorrow though - check out day - I'm sure they'll dispose of everything from this bedroom. I smiled to myself as thoughts of my upcoming evening meandered through my excited mind. It won't be long now.

* * *

A knock at the door. Opened. A vision of beauty. A smile on her face broadened only when I hand her ten, twenty, thirty, forty, fifty, seventy, ninety... Fish in my pocket for another note... One hundred pounds. Notes slid into her handbag. Handbag placed on the table next to the flat-screen television currently advertising an option for express check-out. She turns to me. Business conducted, she thinks, so time for the fun to start. A different idea in my head. One she won't be expecting. No need to rush. Fast forward the small talk. No need to dwell upon words spoken. Only lies. Fake name from me. Most likely Naomi is a fake name too. Lies on both of our parts. She doesn't think I'm cute looking, she doesn't 'dig' the clothes that I'm wearing. In turn, I don't really work in sales and I'm not really here on a business seminar. Clothes on the floor, in a heaped mess. Don't usually permit this but she's prettier than some of the others I've been sent.

Lying on my front, her hands on my back, rubbing. The advert specified a professional massage. A little bit of baby-oil and a quick rub up and down with little to no pressure - hardly a professional massage. As much of a lie as most of the words from her mouth. Hands on my legs, starting behind the knees and running upwards towards my buttocks. Not a horrible sensation but not one that I'll remember when my evening comes to an end and I walk away with a feeling of satisfaction and euphoria at a job well done. Slight whispers in my ear, with me still on my front. Not so much words, more like soft moans. A cheap trick to try and tease and titillate. Stirrings down below. Cheap tricks work. An order to roll onto my back. Order accepted. On my back. The pretty girl with the fake name, straddling me. A gentle rocking motion, grinding down onto my erect penis with only the smallest of g-strings keeping contact to a minimum. A question. Do I want to fuck her? A smile on my face. I want to fuck her; I want to fuck her up. Condom pulled from between breast and bra. Wrapper torn with teeth, rubber sheath pulled from within. A hand on my throbbing shaft keeps it steady. Condom over the head of my cut penis. A quick motion; a rolling downwards. G-string pulled to one side. Smile on her face. Heavy breaths as she grinds her cunt against my covered shaft. A sigh from both of us as she slides me inside as far as I can go. A gentle rocking. Another question. How do I want to fuck her? Easily answered with my hands around her throat.

Eyes bulging. A gasping for air. Desperate clawing. Still inside her as she struggles. A pleasurable feeling. A quick roll. Her on her back. Me on top. Still inside. She's still clawing. The smell of fear. The air of desperation and panic. Her eyes rolling in the back of her head. The smile on my face. The bulging veins on the side of her head. The hands dropping to her side. The final squeeze accompanied with frantic thrusting. A twitch from her finger. The dilation of the pupils. The familiar spasm in my leg. The orgasm. The shudder. The rush. The breathlessness. Collapse. No need to withdraw. No need to move. Enjoy the moment. Share her peace. Checkout isn't until 11am tomorrow morning. We have all night and we're going to need it for I really do believe that, with this canvas, I will truly be able to come up with a masterpiece.

SUNDAY

1.

I collected the assorted letters piled on the doormat and stepped into my cold flat after wishing my neighbour a good morning. As usual they were inquisitive as to where I'd been recently but I fobbed them off with a story about having to visit some relatives up north; a completely different direction to where I really stayed last night. A quick back and forth about how we've both been, some fake smiles - at least on my part - and a suggestion of a catch up soon as it had been a while since we had last ventured out for a drink together.

"Didn't even know you had relatives up north," the neighbour had said to me, eyebrows raised, when I bumped into him in the hallway, as though he believed he knew everything about my life. He didn't. He knew nothing about my world. Just the little easy lies that I occasionally drip fed him to keep him from suspecting I was anything but a normal neighbour. What is normal anyway?

"Haven't seen them for a long time," I told him, my tone as cool as ice. "Family emergency," I stopped myself from giving too much information away. You make the lies too complicated and they have a nasty way of catching up with you and - before you know it - you've talked yourself into a plot filled with messy holes begging to be discovered and questioned. Questions like that can be the end for people such as me. First rule of being good at what I do: Learn to lie. Keep it simple.

"Bit busy at the moment - things to take care of - we'll catch up soon for a drink though?" I told him before he had the chance to ask me further questions or engage in fruitless conversation meant only to waste my time and peak a little into my private life. I'd always make excuses when I encountered him, or any of the other neighbours, as I passed by them outside. A quick excuse to get out of long conversations. Each time I'd only give them enough time to say something along the lines of 'that would be nice' before I was gone. A little smile as I'd slide the key into my door and twist the lock open before stepping in.

Safely in my flat with the door to the outside world closed I threw my overnight bag - filled with spare clothes and a few choice mementos from last night - to the side of the hallway, where it landed with a heavy thud, and went into the lounge. I'd worry about unpacking later, not that it would take me long. With the post in hand I collapsed onto the settee. It had been a long night and although I felt good I was absolutely shattered to the point of almost falling asleep at the wheel of my car - certainly not the best thing to do when you had an overnight bag filled with... That reminded me... I reached into my jacket pocket and pulled out my wallet. A flick of the wrist and the creased leather swung open revealing my credit cards. I say my credit cards but they weren't my credit cards. None of them had my real name on them. My real name? Been so long since I've used it I'm not entirely sure I can remember what it was. I pulled the top card out. Can't use that one again. Need to control my urges better. The first card I managed to obtain and it hadn't even been used to a quarter of the available limit. All I'd used it for was the fish hooks, wire and

- of course - the cash withdrawal for the hotel room. I just made sure I found a shop, in the middle of nowhere, a place where I was sure there were no cameras present to capture my image. I'm not ready for my image to be out there yet. Not until I've finished anyway and then I want the world to know who I am. I enjoyed last night but that's still wasteful. I could have had much more fun utilising this piece of plastic if it weren't for my lack of patience and self-control. An impromptu reaction to an otherwise stressful day. No sense worrying about it now. Besides which there's still a number of unused cards ready and waiting. They were the first thing I got when I realised where my life was headed. Start with the cards and then the tools I'd need and then... Well... too late now. That plan is out of the window due to my career taking a sudden 'quick-start' yesterday.

I threw the card onto the coffee table. I'll cut it up later but if I didn't take it out of my wallet now then there was a good chance I'd forget. I leant back on the sofa and closed my eyes. It had been a long night. A sigh escaped from my mouth. So tired. A little nap won't hurt and then I'll check the news. No sense turning it on now. It's too soon. Later though. Sure something will be mentioned later and I honestly can't wait. Nap now. Celebrate later.

* * *

People lined the streets to see me. A few of them had signs calling for me to be hanged but many of them had smiles on their faces and autograph books in their hands, so it's easy to ignore the ones who protested for my undeserved death. The happy ones though, if they weren't holding autograph books then they clutched at copies of one of the many magazines where I'd hit the front cover. I stood on a red carpet which stretched from the car I'd only just pulled up in - right across to the front of the building I was headed for. A true smile on my face. A pen in my hand as I frantically scribbled my name onto one of the many items I'd been asked to sign.

A wave of people surged forward, albeit slowly, to try and get closer. Some of them called my name. Some of them told me how I was an inspiration, words which brought a smile to my pale face. To the ones who couldn't quite reach me I tried to catch their eyes before giving them a friendly wave. I showed them I appreciated them for coming out to see me although I couldn't get over to speak to them personally. One of my entourage, a large man in a black suit, who was there for my protection as much as the protection of the crowd, urged me to move forward as there were more people waiting to see me inside the building. They could wait though. They weren't going anywhere. Anyway the people out here had been good enough to wait to see me for most of the day. They deserved my attention just as much as the ones inside. I wouldn't ignore anyone. I would never ignore anyone. It wasn't (and isn't) in my nature. I'd worked so hard to be where I was today - I didn't want anyone thinking I wasn't grateful to them for being there. I wanted to see them just as much as they wanted to see me. I lived for this.

Cameras flashed from every direction. Blinding. Despite the distraction they offered I didn't mind them. After all - I'm a bigger picture kind of guy and it just meant there would be more exposure for me tomorrow. Whether it was to be on some fans' Facebook pages or yet more articles in more magazines and newspapers, I was happy with all of the attention. I didn't even mind the negative press. The fact people were out there who deemed it necessary to write such poison about me - well it just showed that, in some way, they cared. More to the point, they were thinking of me. All the time I am in the mind of others - I'm an Immortal. A God among men, women and children. My smile broadened as someone asked me to sign a magazine cover but to make it out to their mum instead of their own name. They loved my work but their mother loved it more apparently. I could get used to this. She would have been there herself but the face in the crowd explained she was in hospital having had emergency surgery to remove a burst appendix. I nodded as though I cared and told the face that I hoped her mother would make a speedy recovery. Truth be told, though, I couldn't care less. I didn't want to hear their life stories. I just wanted to hear how much they loved me. Couldn't say that though. Didn't want to turn the faces away from me. I needed to keep up the caring routine and, despite the hand on my back, which gently pushed me forward I asked the face whether they had a mobile phone. They nodded. Call your mum, I suggested. They did. I took the phone and had a charming conversation with what sounded to be an elderly lady. She was, supposedly, my biggest fan. I heard that a lot. I always wondered which of them is truly my biggest fan? She liked the fact that my work served two purposes; both of which were equally important. On the one hand it helped rid the world of the parasites who darkened our days and, on the other hand, the art was beautiful. She explained how she felt it had taken Damien Hirst's idea (with the cutting in half of the cow) and taken it to the next (necessary) level. I thanked her for her kind words. Little did she know, Damien Hirst was my inspiration. Him and my father (but it was more to do with just wanting to prove to the latter that I could achieve what he had failed to do - get recognition for my art where his went mostly unseen). I told her that without people like her, who urged me to continue, I'd be nothing. She told me that could never be the case. I was destined for greatness and I was already mostly there. Her words, not mine. I felt myself blush but didn't disagree with her. Why would I? I didn't catch her name so I asked. Jackie. I wished her the best of health and handed her back to her child who was patiently waiting. She immediately started to scream down the phone. I moved further down the line but could still hear the excitement from the pair of them - neither could believe I'd taken the time to have a phone conversation during the busy evening. More cameras flashed than before. It wasn't just the mother and her child who were suitably impressed. My actions seemed to please the others too who were now frantically waving their own phones in my face. There'd definitely be more stories of me tomorrow and I looked forward to them.

* * *

I woke up with a smile on my face. A pleasant dream. It made a nice change. Usually I have night terrors of the worst kind. I guess it had something to do with my evening. I hope the quietness and the good dreams last forever because I have a feeling the darkness will be back, once again, as memories of last night fade away. Rested, I stood up and walked into the hallway. I picked up the bag and carried it through to the kitchen. I put it on the side and turned the kettle on after filling it. Nice to see a tap that's not coated in lime scale. I opened the bag and reached in. A quick fish around before I pulled out some Polaroid photographs. Souvenirs of the previous night; multiple pictures of the scene I'd left for the maid to find and - more importantly - the press. I smiled as I cast my eyes over the pictures and relived those moments.

* * *

After death, I inserted hooks into the girl's wrists and ankles. My technique had been honed on pieces of meat from the butcher local to my old family home, out in the country. Sharp hooks which I'd bought with the fake credit card from a sports shop miles from where I lived. No chance of being recognised. The hooks I buy are the ones meant for catching large fish in rough seas. Once they pierced the girl's still-warm skin I'd taken the strongest fishing wire you could get and attached it to the corner of the room. Wire from her left wrist and ankle attached to the left corners of the room (thanks to multiple vine eye hooks in the corners of the room and a 'do not disturb sign' on the door), wire from the other wrist and ankle to the right. It was tricky but entirely possible to suspend the girl from the floor. I preferred to have them facing downwards. It looked more dramatic than having them looking up. Another reason why I didn't like them pointing that way was because it also made it impossible for police officers to see the face until they'd cut her down and I preferred them to see it as soon as they walked in. I believe it added more drama to the scene. Once the girl had been hung I'd taken a large knife from my overnight bag, carefully wrapped up in a shirt.

With the tip of its blade I'd cut from her throat down to her navel; a messy procedure but one which allowed for her intestines to drop to the floor in a puddle of delightful gore. One which excited me. From there I'd patiently taken the time to rearrange them into a pattern which suited my mood. In this instance it was a snail-shell, the guts going round and round in a neat little series of circles spiralling inwards to the middle. Only when that was done did I take the time to step back and admire my work. A feeling of euphoria washed over me, followed by a smile spreading across my face. I reached for my camera and took pictures. The Polaroid's weren't a necessity of course: such a work of art would be hard to forget but - even so - I wanted to collect them. I wanted to have something to look back upon, in my darker days, in an effort to cheer myself up from one of my moods.

When morning came my heart was beating ten to the dozen. Panic was starting to set in. I hadn't been ready to do... I looked at the scene... all this. I hadn't been ready. Had I really made sure as to clean all my DNA from the scene? Had I cleaned enough? Left no trace of myself? Did they have cameras in the hotel? Had they got my image? I shook away the self-doubt and straightened up. I can't think of this now. I can't. I need to get out of here before the maid comes a knocking.

One final look at the scene. I did well. I can't wait to hear the reactions.

* * *

I put the photos to one side. The first of what I hope will be many mementos as I explore my hobby further; I'll start an album with these later. At least as long as I don't get caught after this one. I was pretty sure I'd covered all my bases. I was proud of what I had achieved but, even so, the loss of control and impatience... that wasn't good.

I checked the time on my old wrist watch with its fraying leather strap. I hadn't realised I'd dozed for so long. A good solid few hours. One downside was that it would make it harder to sleep through the night later on, when I'm wishing slumber would take a hold. On the plus-side - I'm betting I must be on every news channel now - and not just the local news either. The perks of modern technology for you; news travels fast. Why, I bet word had already spread to continents far across the oceans. People would already know of my stage-name - the one I'd inked on the wall of the hotel room before leaving, using droplets of the whore's blood as ink.

I stretched across the sofa and reached for the remote control sitting on its tatty arm. Turning the television on, I started flicking through the channels. I hadn't even found a news station yet, but my heart raced with anticipation. This is it. This is my moment. This is my introduction to the world. I only hope they're ready for me but then, if they're not, I won't be the first artist to have been misunderstood.

SUNDAY

2.

The shrill scream of the alarm told me the all-too-brief weekend was over, and it's the start of another monotonous day. I squinted at the digital display as I silenced the bloody thing, and took a moment just to get my head together. Part of me seriously considered rolling over and going back to sleep, but just as quickly, I dismissed the idea. Under the circumstances, I can't afford another sick day.

As I dragged myself out of bed it dawned on me, not for the first time, just how old I'm starting to feel. It's a sneaky bastard that old age, creeping up on me without warning. On my way to the bathroom, the same old routine took over my tired and fuzzy brain. I stepped over the floorboards that I knew would creak. I peeked out of the window to witness the dawning of another overcast, dreary day. I washed and brushed my teeth, attempting to ignore the signs that Father Time is starting to give me a damn good kicking. It's funny, because I struggle to see that fresh-faced officer who joined the police force all those years ago. The shine in the eyes has dulled, the cheeks have started to jowl, and the hair that was once thick and black is starting to thin and go gray at the edges.

Thanks, Father Time. Thanks a lot.

I didn't bother to shave, as I couldn't be arsed. Instead, I headed to the kitchen and made a coffee, enjoying the solitude, for a while at least.

See, the chance to think reminds me of all the things that the day job helps me to ignore. I hate my job. *Hate* it. I was naïve enough to think that I would be something special, that as soon as I made detective I could change the world. If only I could meet that younger version of myself now: I would slap him, shake him by the shoulders, and tell him that in the grand scheme of things, Martin Andrews would not make much of an impact on the complex and depressingly active world of serious crime.

The problem is that it is too deeply ingrained into society. Kids as young as seven or eight are on street corners dealing drugs, some of them armed with guns bought from back-street dealers. The majority of the public don't see this of course. To them, we keep them safe and secure.

What a fucking joke.

The fact is we're overstretched, and it's often easier to sweep a lot of crimes - the robberies and muggings, the domestic assaults and vandalisms - under the carpet. At least that was how it used to be.

My eyes drifted to the small black and white photo on the fridge held in place by magnets. That fuzzy squiggle changed my outlook.

Kids will do that.

It didn't seem real until Lucy started to show, but as her stomach grew, so did my concerns. What kind of world is this to bring a kid into?

Don't get me wrong, I'm ecstatic. Over the moon to be a father. I just don't know if the world as it is right now is somewhere for my kid to be able to live a good and safe life. I suppose it's something that all police officers feel, especially the ones like me who know how much stuff goes both unsolved and unreported. I know guys who have been falsifying reports and documentation for years, all because they need to meet targets, make sure the funding comes for another year. It's a tightrope. A fucking tightrope.

Still, moping around and feeling sorry for myself won't help. All I can do is promise myself that I'll stop being lazy, and make sure that I get as many of the scum off the streets before my new son or daughter comes into this world.

Will it make any difference?

In the grand scheme of things, probably not. Nevertheless, I have to try, if only for my own peace of mind. Tired of moping and dwelling on what might be, I decided to head in to the office early. Maybe I'd stop at the McDonalds drive-through on the way for an Egg Mcmuffin. My doctor says I have to watch my stress levels and cholesterol, but in this instance, I was willing to ignore his advice. It's Sunday after all, and I needed something to give me a little pick up before another shitty week begins.

* * *

Art

The drive into work was predictably frustrating. Even at this time on a Sunday morning, the roads were gridlocked with church-goers and taxi drivers who seemed to operate from a different highway code to the rest of us. I didn't even have the pleasure of eating my Egg McMuffin due to the line at the drive in stretching for what looked like a quarter of a mile. Fuck it, I'll grab something later. I could almost see my doctor's smug face as I crawled past the turnoff and the inviting golden arches sign.

Eventually, I arrived at work. To see that ugly gray concrete building set against the equally gray sky made my heart sink just a little. As usual, all of the good parking spaces were taken, so I drove my shitty little Ford Escort to the back of the car park and pulled in. The cold bit hard and whipped my jacket against my body as I made my way to the building. It's only the start of November, and already freezing most mornings. I have a feeling it's going to be a bitch of a winter, which seems a little unfair considering that, as usual, we had no summer to speak of. I pushed my way into the building, wrinkling my nose at stale smell of old polish. Fortunately, reception was empty. It seems even the drunks and other assorted dickheads that usually populate it hadn't yet dragged themselves out of their pits for long enough to cause trouble. It was the first good news of the day as I punched in my key code and walked through the 'staff only' door.

Serious crimes is up on the third floor. It's easy enough to walk up the steps, but I was feeling particularly lazy today, so I called the lift.

As I waited, I saw Perkins saunter over. He's only a year out of the academy, and although he's a good kid, I really couldn't be arsed with him this morning.

"Shit the bed Martin?" he said, grinning at me as he came close.

He reminded me of myself when I was young. He has that same brightness in his eyes. I half-considered telling him to do something else with his life before it's too late, but that also sounded like too much effort, so I simply smiled back.

"Thought I'd come in early, catch up on some paperwork. What are you doing here?"

"Just been to the gym. I like to get an hour or so in before I start work."

I nodded and sucked my gut in at the same time.

"Good idea. Family all okay?" I asked him whilst praying for the lift to hurry itself up.

"Can't complain. You? Any sign of that rug rat yet?"

"Not yet, shouldn't be long though." I replied as I stared at the door to the stairs, wondering if I could make a good enough excuse to get away from this conversation.

"Make the most of it, you won't get any sleep once it arrives." He said, flashing his perfect grin.

A couple of thoughts entered my head at that instant. The first was that Perkins was probably one of those guys who went through a lot of women. The second thought was to maybe tell him that I barely slept now as it was because I was worried about so many things. I opened my mouth to give some kind of non-committal comment when the doors chimed, and my escape route opened.

"This is me. I'll speak to you later, Perkins."

I strode into the lift and pressed the button for my floor before he could answer. I could see he was a little put out, but frankly, I couldn't have cared less. I've bigger things to worry about than offending Dale Perkins.

I'd hoped to find the third floor empty, but to my surprise, there were already a lot of people up there who genuinely looked busy. I strode towards my super - a big jowly old buzzard by the name of Patterson.

"Ah, Andrews, I was just about to ring you at home," he said, turning towards me. He always looked serious, but this time his frown was a little bit deeper than normal.

"What's going on?"

"Murder."

"Another great start to the morning eh?"

I grinned, but Patterson remained impassive. Something didn't seem right, and I let the grin fall from my face and gave my full attention to the boss.

"This is a bad one Martin. Really bad."

I nodded, I'd never seen him so flustered, and that made me wonder if my bad day was about to get worse.

"What happened?"

"Some poor girl has been ripped up in a hotel room."

"Where did it happen?"

"Crummy little place on the outskirts of the city. We're heading out there now. Forensics are on their way. You can ride with me if you want."

"Its fine, I'll follow you in my own car." I said, thinking that company other than my own was probably a bad idea.

"Suit yourself. Come on then, let's get gone."

The hotel was already taped off when we arrived. It was one of those lower mid-range ones, the kind of place that liked to kid itself that it was luxury, but would no doubt have its share of damp patches and suspect stains on the bedding. I got out of the car, crossing to and ducking under the tape as I headed inside out of the drizzle. I could feel a headache coming on and wanted to deal with this as quickly as I could. The need for nicotine gnawed at my guts, but I'd promised Lucy I would quit when she found out about the baby, and I wasn't about to give in if I could help it. I pushed my addiction aside and walked with Patterson into the lobby.

It was unspectacular. Green furnishings, ugly maroon carpet which was a good five years past its best, cheap reproduction paintings on the wall. It wasn't quite a place that charged by the hour, but at the same time, I couldn't see it winning any awards for cleanliness. I fell in beside Patterson as he led the way.

"The maid found the body this morning when she went in to turn the room. Whoever did it really took their time."

"Is anyone tracing the check in I.D?"

"We are, but I don't expect to find anything. When you see the trouble this prick went to, you'll see why."

What about payment method? Are we lucky enough to hope for a credit card?"

Patterson shook his head. "Paid with cash. He was careful."

"What about CCTV?"

Patterson snorted and raised his eyebrows. "In a place like this? No chance. I'm guessing that's why he picked it in the first place. Hotels like this one don't tend to ask too many questions of their clientele."

We bypassed the lift and went into a small office tucked out of the way by the bar. The maid who had found the body sat at the table, cradling a cup of coffee. I knew she was the one who'd discovered the body because she had that look in her eyes that all witnesses did. I'd seen it before when death sprang up unexpectedly and slapped someone in the face: Car crashes; The unexpected suicides of loved ones; Robberies where somebody's mother, brother or father had happened to be in the wrong place at the wrong time and had found themselves on the end of a bullet.

Yes. This was an all too familiar sight in this job. The poor woman's eyes were haunted and devoid of understanding as she tried to make sense of whatever she had seen. She carried that haunted vacancy that came with seeing the reality of death up close. It would never leave her, the image of the things she had seen. I envied her for being so unaccustomed, and wouldn't wish a discovery like that on anyone. She looked me in the eye, looking for something. Some words that would make it better, some comfort that would make those awful images vacate her mind. The truth was there were none, at least not that I knew of anyway. The best thing for her would be time. Unfortunately, it wasn't a luxury I could give her.

It was important to get as much information as possible whilst it was still fresh. The human brain tends to embellish and add more things that never actually happened the longer it is left alone to think about it. It's not the fault of the witness – or at least in most cases it isn't – but the fact was I needed to get the info right away before she could forget or change it enough to make it useless. At least things are better than they used to be. Since Cognitive interviewing had become standard practice back in the eighties, there was less chance of getting bad information. Even so, it was still up to me to ask the right questions in the right way to get results. Call me a manipulative bastard, but it was my job.

I sat opposite her as Patterson hovered and placated the hotel manager, who was growing increasingly worried about the extensive police presence outside the hotel and how it might impact his business. Pushing his high pitch squeaks to the same 'come back later' part of my brain where I'd sent the nicotine craving, I turned my attention back to the maid.

She was eastern European, late thirties by the looks of things. Her skin was pale, but I'm not sure if that was due to the shock of finding a body or natural. She had an ugly wart on her cheek which I forced myself not to stare at. Instead I held her gaze, and tried to not to let the vacant horror I saw there bother me.

"I'm detective Martin Andrews," I said, giving her the professional script. "I need to ask you a few questions if you feel up to answering them."

The woman stared right through me, mouth partially agape. I wasn't holding out hope of her being much use yet, but I had procedure to follow, so I asked her what happened.

"On Okazywał jej," she whispered, looking at me with pleading eyes seeking a reassurance that I didn't have the power to give.

"I don't understand, please, tell me what happened."

"On Okazywał jej!" She repeated, this time spitting out the words in her native tongue.

I glanced over to Patterson, eyebrows raised.

"Get her to write it down,"

I pulled a notepad out of my jacket and pushed it toward her, handing her a tatty biro that I kept meaning to replace. She set aside her coffee and copied it down. It made just as little sense on paper, but I knew what to do. I pulled out my phone and punched up Google. Bless the internet. Amid the pictures of funny dogs and pages and pages of useless shit, there were actually some useful services. I keyed the text into an online translation service and waited until it made a bridge between our languages. The results came back almost instantly, and as I read them, I wondered just what had happened here.

"What does it say?" Patterson asked.

I held out my phone to him so he could read it for himself.

"Christ, I think we better go up to the room and take a look."

"Want me to stay here and continue the interview?" I asked.

"No, you come up with me. You always have a good eye for stuff like this. I'll send Richards in to finish the interview."

"Got it," I said, happy to be off the hook as far as having to ask all those mind-numbingly repetitious questions while secretly looking forward to getting back to the station so I could wash some pills down with coffee to try and catch this headache. On my notepad, just below the maid's scrawled words, I penned in the translation in case I needed it later.

On Okazywał jej.

He displayed her.

I got up and followed Patterson to the lift. It was time we went to see what we were dealing with.

The ride up to the sixth floor was the exact opposite of my wait for the lift at the station. This time, it wasn't a case of wishing the ride would go quicker, it was a dull sense of dread and the hope that it might never end. The doors chimed, and I stepped from sticky carpet onto worn hotel corridor. I could see the room at the end of the hall, or more specifically, the officer outside the door. Patterson and I headed towards it. It was interesting that he seemed to be in about as much of a rush as I was. Maybe there was something in this police instinct thing and he sensed it too.

We reached the door and looked inside, and two things were immediately apparent. First, this was definitely not something we would be able to sweep away, and second, that I was glad I'd missed out on eating that morning. As it was, my stomach rolled as I looked at the scene beyond the door. It seemed the maid was spot on in her assessment.

Something awful had happened here. And, whoever was responsible, had indeed displayed her.

"Jesus," Patterson whispered. "We need to get a lid on this right now. No press. If this leaks, there'll be a frenzy."

I could only nod. Partly because of the morbid fascination at what confronted us, and partly because this was the exact reason why I didn't want to bring a kid into the world.

I glanced at Patterson, then the two of us entered the room.

MONDAY

3.

Monday morning and I awoke with the winter's rain hammering down hard against the double-glazed window. I felt emotionally drained - a feeling which surprised me after the fun I'd had on Saturday evening whilst creating my masterpiece. Monday morning. The weekend already feels so long ago. The excitement of Saturday night followed by the harsh disappointment of a wet and miserable Sunday; a day which I'd filled by watching various news programs whilst still beating myself up over my loss of control. Yes, the scene was good. The Art I had left was beautiful. I can't help but think, though, that it could have been even better.

Some of the news programmes had been local and some were national. Each time I stumbled across one of the broadcasts I felt my excitement rise as I expected to hear about my art but each time there was nothing. It was almost as though I'd been completely ignored. The worst feeling for any person of a creative mindset. We're there, shouting for the world to notice us and yet they continue to walk on by as though we're completely invisible. To everyone else we simply didn't exist.

I was standing in front of the bathroom mirror half-dressed for work in my brown uniform of shirt and trousers. Name badge for Damon Benton on the left hand pocket. My third fake name if memory serves me right. I already looked tired and my week hadn't properly started yet. There were large black bags under my eyes from a night filled with continually disturbed sleep and I had a five o'clock shadow, darker than usual, from where I hadn't bothered shaving. Had it not been for the fact I enjoyed my job, I'd have been tempted to call in sick. Had I done so then it would have been the first sick day I'd ever taken from this company. I sighed as I buttoned my shirt and stepped out of the bathroom, closing the door behind me. It's a good job I enjoyed my work - nearly as much as the darkness within me enjoyed it when I let it loose.

The drive to work was spent flicking through radio stations. After the media silence of Sunday, I didn't expect to stumble upon anything but - even so - a small part of me remained hopeful. Every time the news came on I'd wait until the broadcast had finished before continuing my search for the next news announcement. Of the six stations programmed into my car, I managed to catch the news on three separate occasions. None of them mentioned the artwork I'd produced in the hotel. It was hard to pretend I wasn't annoyed. Words couldn't actually describe exactly how ticked off I was. I'd felt so sure that Saturday would have been the start of my other career (despite being ahead of schedule). I wasn't stupid. I knew Saturday evening was a spur of the moment kind of thing but the act itself had been well practised and thought through. I'd pictured how the following morning was going play out so many times in my mind. The maid would have gone into the room and seen the display. Ignorant of the fact she was looking at a piece of art she'd scream at the sight of the body. It would alert people in rooms nearby who would come and investigate for themselves. They too would scream. Maybe some of them would even pass out? Naturally it wouldn't have been long before the police were called. They'd be shocked initially but eventually come to realise there was actually meaning behind what they were seeing. Someone, somewhere, would get a picture on their phone - the world we live in today dictates as much. The picture would get leaked to the press. The world would see my art. My alter-ego would be famous overnight.

Now that's how it should have worked out so what the hell went wrong? Just because the hotel was slightly shabby, it was still getting customers frequenting it and the reviews online were also near on perfect, so that ruled out the possibility that the art had remained undiscovered because the maids had yet to clean out the room or because the room hadn't been booked since. I mean, if I'd chosen a bottom of the range hotel in the middle of nowhere - the kind that rarely gets any visitors... well then I would have understood it going undiscovered for a couple of days. But in this hotel? Not a chance. Someone had stumbled upon it. Not just one person. A number of people would have seen it by now. The maid, the hotel management, a handful of lucky guests, a number of police officers, the forensics team and surely some members of the press - they would have all seen it by now.

Twenty five minutes after leaving home I turned into my workplace's car park. Unlike other people I don't bother driving up and down in the hope of finding a space close to the building's doors. That's just lazy and, besides which, when it comes time to leave it just means they have to queue to get out. I simply pull into the first one I come across even if it's obvious there are more spaces further up which would require less walking.

I turned the engine off and sat there for a moment, still quietly stewing over the lack of media coverage. I felt deflated. Ignore it, I thought. Push it to one side. I can't let people see this side of me. It goes against the character I've created for myself here. I need to put the mask of happiness on. I took a deep breath, opened the door and climbed out of the warmth of my car, the cold air hitting me instantly. I hated the winter as much as I hated being ignored. I shook the thoughts from my mind as I spotted a work colleague getting out of their own car.

"Morning," I called out - a perfect fake smile on my face.

The building's manager had just pulled up in his large, expensive car. We would always arrive at the same time. He never smiled in return, and neither would he reply. I didn't expect anything but nevertheless his blatant ignorance bothered me immensely. Manners cost nothing and if someone like me can afford to be polite to my neighbours, on a near daily basis, then someone like him should have no excuse to ignore me. Besides, engaging other people in conversation, even if basic and brief, is always good practice for me. It ensures I remember to keep my happy face on. The mask I hide behind. But the day I turn around and tell him to fuck himself, the day I stab him in the neck with my car keys - that's the day I'll go home again and phone in sick.

As per usual the friendly greeting went unanswered and as per usual I acted like I didn't care. Instead I pretended I'd left something in the car and turned back. I leaned in through the door and counted down from twenty. There was nothing in there that I needed - it was just my way of ensuring I didn't have to walk in with the boss with an awkward silence between us which I feared would encourage the darkness within my damaged soul to crawl out. In plain sight - I'm not sure I could have controlled it. I'd probably end up smashing his face onto one of the concrete steps by the front door, then joyfully stamping upon the back of his head with a maniacal grin splattered across my face. All I can think is thank God he wasn't my manager. I worked in a different department. Security. I had my own boss to answer to and thankfully he was nicer than this douche.

My boss, Gary, greeted me the same way, every Monday. An elderly man, one year past his retirement, who continued to work full-time because he enjoyed it. He'd always ask if I'd had a good weekend. I'd always say yes even if it had been a disappointment. I'd then enquire as to how his had been. The answer was always the same too; a round or two of golf and that he certainly couldn't complain. He would then go one way on his patrols and I'd go the other. We wouldn't speak again until the following morning or if we happened to bump into each other in the staff room at lunch time.

I entered the building via the gallery's visitors' door. One of my colleagues waited, unlocking the door to let the staff in then locking it again. I've often wondered whether it would be cheaper for the company to just cut us our own keys cut rather than pay a someone to do it, but I guess it's all down to keeping the building more secure. Fewer key-holders equals fewer opportunities for potential theft.

The smell hit me instantly, reminding me of my old school. It was a strange scent, which you both hate and love simultaneously;

33

cleaning products mixed with the stink of old, over-used text books, and chalk dust tainted with the hint of aftershave and perfume. A small gift shop stood to the left of the doors - selling replicas of the paintings displayed in the gallery, for a fair price, along with other tackier merchandise like mugs and key-chains. I rarely saw people buy from the little shop, though. Part of me wondered how much longer they'd bother to keep it open. Admission booth was to the right of the building's entrance, next to the cloakrooms with Security directly in front of the doors. You'd think that, given what I did over my weekend, security and such would make me nervous but I liked these people. Six of them in total. Three on each day. They rota'd who worked with whom and they all seemed genuinely pleasant but it wasn't their mannerisms or personalities that I appreciated. It's the job they did. They kept the art safe - just as I did with my daily patrols. I mean, yes, they're here for the safety of the visitors too - as was I - but their main goal was to keep the art secure. I walked past the security with no issues, a slight nod of my head to acknowledge their presence, and continued past the first corridor towards the locker room upstairs.

People ask how I can do this job; standing around for hours on end looking at the same displays whilst pointing people in the right direction if they get lost. Being vigilant to any wrong-doing - such as people touching the paintings or sculptures or just being loud and obnoxious... the usual anti-social behaviour, not that you see a lot of it here. I guess this isn't the sort of establishment which attracts that sort of crowd. Not that I mind. I like the quieter crowds that come here. People who enjoy looking at ancient artefacts, paintings and such. I don't really have to get involved with people, other than the odd smile and general assistance. I can stand around in the open and yet completely blend into the environment. People think it's a boring job with days dragging on forever but I enjoy it. Hours spent looking at pictures I've seen a thousand times before. Displays I never tire of. Every time I look at them I see something I've not seen before; always spotting something new. It's like my home from home and I love it. I love the customers too because they have an appreciation for what's on display, a fascination which I share and understand. My only wish is that we housed Damien Hirst's work here. I can't get the cow-piece out of my mind. It's good but not beautiful. The inside of a cow is just ugly. Fascinating, but ugly. Not like the human body. *That* is beautiful. That needs to be seen. Because it's art - *God's* art. He made us all beautiful inside (organ-wise at least).

It was just a shame that most of us weren't beautiful on the outside too but then, if that were the case, who would I use for my pieces?

* * *

"Good morning, young man!" Gary called to me as soon as I stepped into the locker room. "Did you have a good weekend?"

I smiled. Not at him but rather at his predictability. "I did thank you,"

"That's good!" He pulled his name badge from his locker and stuck it to his shirt at chest level.

"How was your weekend?" I asked.

"It was a cold one," he said, "but I managed to fit in a couple of rounds of golf so I can't complain."

Once again I found myself smiling at his predictability. "Is there ever a time where you don't play golf?"

Gary closed his locker door, securing it tightly. He smiled at me. "You're not married are you?" he asked. I shook my head. "Well - when you're married you'll understand why I get out to the golf course as much as I possibly can," he said, "and - what's more - you'll realise why I won't take retirement!" He laughed - as did I, although it was the mask I wore that was laughing. "Anyway," he continued, "you have a good day!" He walked out of the room.

"You too," I answered, as he disappeared into the corridor. The door slammed shut and the smile disappeared from my face.

I've often wondered why people bother to get married. Whenever I overhear couples talking, whilst out and about, they never sound as though they're entirely happy. It's always like one of them is being nagged or is in a mood with the other. And here's Gary - he'd rather continue to work than go home because he knows his wife is waiting for him. Sure he could be joking but going from what I've seen of couples - and the way he is in general - I think he's being serious. I wonder how he'd react if I were to offer him the chance for his wife to be part of my up-and-coming collection.

The smile slowly crept across my face as I considered what I'd do to his wife. He would occasionally make a comment to the effect that she'd go around with her head up her arse. He would ask her what was wrong and she'd reply she was fine. In my mind, I was wondering whether I could actually force her decapitated head up her rectum. I closed the little door and locked it up before putting the key in my pocket. I'll make a note of that image on my lunch-break. It might come in handy some time.

And so begins another day.

MONDAY

4.

My days are usually filled with people-watching and looking at the exhibits but today was different. Today was - well - today was a let-down. I was supposed to be in my element. This was supposed to be the start of my new life. The way I pictured it - I was meant to be surrounded by items that I love, people that I enjoy watching coupled with thoughts of my weekend and - specifically - what people must be thinking of it all. Some of them sickened by what I'd done and some of them fascinated. Instead I felt as though I wasn't here. I felt as though my weekend never happened. I felt... I felt out of sorts. It was supposed to shock people and make them take note. It was supposed to reach across the world but it seemed as though my efforts didn't even reach the front desk of the hotel lobby. Maybe my work just hasn't been understood yet? Maybe it hasn't been truly appreciated for what it actually is? I won't be the first artist in the world not to have my talents truly recognised until years later. Not that I want to wait. Anyway I shouldn't have to wait. Not in today's world. My fame or infamy - I'm fine with either - should have been almost instantaneous.

As I sat here in the near-empty staffroom, watching my colleagues flicking their way through the daily newspapers whilst eating their tuna sandwiches with more noise than entirely necessary, I couldn't help but wonder whether today's world is a little *too* used to violent imagery and sickening scenes. A broken world desensitised to the violence which once haunted its dreams. Maybe. Maybe not.

Maybe I chose the wrong hotel. Maybe it was as simple as that. Perhaps the guests are used to seeing previous occupants being left like that? Should have gone to the Hilton. Paid that little bit extra. Unless - yes, maybe that's it - perhaps the manager of the hotel didn't want the scene to have an impact on his business and after the maid had reported what she'd seen he'd simply told her to clean it up before anyone else saw. I somehow doubt it but at least it would explain the silence. Besides, any good manager would surely know it would add revenue to their business. The horror-lovers and the art critics would all be wanting to stay in the room where I had originally displayed Naomi. And there's an added bonus too. When news leaks of the woman's profession - the fact she was a whore - other prostitutes would be reluctant to visit the establishment for fear of a copycat-style sculpture being made out of them. Already - without even trying very hard - my art had made the hotel an even classier place. Hell, the manager should be thanking me.

I felt the rage building within me. I couldn't believe I was being ignored. I hate being ignored. I deliberately shook the feeling from my mind. I can't afford to let my mask slip. I smiled at my colleague as he looks up at me from his newspaper and half-eaten tuna sandwich, no doubt to see what I was shaking my head at. He smiled back and promptly returned to his own business.

"Anything good in the news today?" I asked him. I hoped he'd tell me what I wanted to hear. I hoped he'd tell me about the hotel room.

"Is there ever anything good in the news?" he replied -

splattering the table in front of him with little pieces of chewed up tuna. "I don't know why I read these - they only depress me." He closed the paper and folded it in two.

"May I?" I asked - another flash of my pearly whites to show him that I'm the sort of person you'd want to share your newspaper with.

"Knock yourself out." He passed the paper across to me and I thanked him. Instantly I unfolded it, on my own table, and saw that the headlines were nothing to do with me, some bullshit I couldn't care less about. A politician caught with his pants down. When aren't they caught like that? I don't even skim read it. I really couldn't care less what goes on in their world. I wildly flicked through to the second page as my colleague said goodbye to me and left the room. I ignored him too. He's about as important in my life as the politicians. I've got what I wanted from him. No need to be polite now. Even less of a reason considering we're not part of the same team.

Damn.

Nothing on the second page either. The third page is a pair of breasts - some naked teen with her thoughts about some kind of current affair. I snorted. The look of this girl - blonde and stupid - told me all I needed to know about her thoughts on current affairs; nothing. She has no mind of her own. The words printed next to her pert breasts were nothing more than the editor's own pointless ramblings. This page served no purpose. The only reason this page had been included was to get sales from horny teens who were too embarrassed to buy a pornographic magazine. Too embarrassed or too young - this was their only chance to see some tits. And those breasts... my disappointed lip curled into a smile. They'd look great stuck to a wall. Just the breasts. Perhaps a wooden frame around them? Now that's sexy.

I turned to page four and then five. Nothing. At least nothing important. Nothing about me. The same goes for pages six, seven and eight. In fact, a quick flick through the rest of the paper showed nothing about what I did with my weekend anywhere. I closed the paper and threw it across the room.

Fuck.

Everything would have been so much easier had I been doing this in the eighties. The only artist in this country - that I can remember at least - was Peter Sutcliffe and Sutcliffe was a pussy. Okay, fine, if the world really has changed, if people really have switched off from such violent imagery, then I'll simply have to up my game. I should take this as a blessing. See Saturday night as a practice run. Come out, in the press, with something even more spectacular. Art that people will not be able to ignore and, more to the point, a vision which will haunt them for the rest of their lives.

I felt a sudden burst of energy surge through me. I started this lunch break feeling deflated but now I'm excited again. I'll use the rest of my afternoon - walking around wearing my mask - taking in the paintings. See if I can pick anything up from them. Some more styles or something to incorporate into my own work and then - tonight - I'll sit down and start planning. I stood up, picked up my trash, and dropped it in the small bin in the corner of the room. Yes. I'm feeling good, definitely more positive. I'd had a good practice run at the weekend, I'd got away with it and now I have time to plan something truly amazing.

I have a feeling that, soon, the world will regret ignoring my original piece.

* * *

My work colleagues must have thought I was Jekyll and Hyde today. I'd been miserable right up until lunch time - my thoughts looping on the feeling of being ignored and my work failing to make so much as a ripple in this messed up world. And then, after lunch, I'd even found myself whistling as I walked from room to room, taking in the paintings and the few people who had chosen to visit the museum on this bitter day. I couldn't help but stand there, in the corner of the room, watching their expressions as they tried to make sense of what the artist had created. I wondered whether they'd have the same look as they viewed my own work; a look of both curiosity and appreciation for what I'd done.

I walked into the locker room and opened mine up. I pulled the name badge from my shirt, dropping it onto a small shelf inside before taking my keys and wallet out. I slipped them into my pocket and reached into the back for my coat.

"Off home then?" Gary made me jump as he came into the room. I was surprised he was still there. Normally he'd have gone home by now.

"I am indeed." I told him. I didn't try and engage him in conversation this time. I was ready to go and my mind was pre-occupied as to how I could take my hobby to the next level; the level that would get me noticed.

"Me too. Been a long day talking with management," he said. He sounded glum but, again, I didn't really dwell on it. "Probably have a large whiskey tonight," he said. "What are your plans?" I tried not to smile as I contemplated as to how I should answer him. "Doing anything nice?"

"Probably just a bit of painting or sketching," I told him. He didn't need to know what I'd really be doing. A clever answer, I thought, because it made me sound more like a person who'd enjoy working in a gallery. Someone with a real passion for the work and someone who wants to be an artist themselves.

"Ah," said Gary, "you fancy yourself a bit of a painter?" he laughed. "Who knows? Maybe one day we'll be watching over *your* work whilst people come in to look at it."

I smiled again. "I do hope so," I said. "I do hope so, indeed." Before he could engage with me further, I exited the room. The door slammed shut behind me. "I really do hope so."

TUESDAY

5.

The morning of Tuesday was spent pretty much the same way as Monday had ended. We went over evidence, looked at photographs for the hundredth time, hoping to see something different; hoping for a break. I knew pretty much from the off that we wouldn't find anything. As ghastly as it was, the scene was set up too perfectly for the killer to make some amateur mistake like checking in using his own name or paying by card. This guy, whoever he was, was a different beast altogether. Or maybe he was just lucky – it was still too early to tell.

Patterson had been rattling on for almost an hour now about chasing down every lead, as if we didn't know how to do our jobs. Truth be told, I had half zoned him out, and had been watching the clock since eleven. I craved a lunchtime slug of alcohol, just something to take the edge off what was beginning to look like a bastard of a workload for the next few weeks.

"Right," he said, perhaps noting our jaded stares. "Let's leave it there and grab some food. This afternoon I want Richards and Wyatt reviewing the rest of the security footage from the building opposite the hotel. Our guy must be on there somewhere."

I pushed myself down in my seat, hoping that he wouldn't single me out for something as shitty and mundane as poor Richards and Wyatt.

"Martin, I want you to take Perkins and go back to the hotel. Question the staff again."

"We already questioned them boss," I said, hoping to get out of an afternoon with the ever irritating Perkins.

"They might have remembered something since then. Just do it to make sure we've covered every angle. I want this prick caught."

I nodded. For once I agreed. I glanced over to Perkins to find him staring at me with that dopey grin on his face. I had a feeling it was going to be a long afternoon. First things first though. That lunchtime pint was calling me, and if I had an afternoon of irritation ahead, I at least wanted to get some drink down my neck first.

* * *

The Red Lion was just down the road from the station. It was convenient, and most afternoons you would find more than a few of my fellow officers there. I walked in to the inviting clack of the pool tables, and the not too loud hum of the jukebox as it played whatever shit passed for music these days. I strode up to the bar, Perkins in tow despite my best efforts to put him off. A couple of the other lads had come along too, and I wondered if the mess that we'd seen had maybe hit us harder than we'd thought. I ordered my poison, a lovely pint of ice cold Tetley's smooth flow. Perkins was hovering, and being either the mug or good Samaritan that I am, I offered to buy him a drink. I wondered what he would order. Tap water? Babycham? Soft drink? To my surprise, he went for Carlsberg, and we made for the corner table where Richards and Wyatt were already waiting.

"Martin. Perkins," Wyatt said as we took our seats. I nodded, marvelling at just how orange the Scottish prick's hair looked in the direct sunlight with the window at his back.

Richards had already necked half his pint, and didn't seem to be at all happy that he would be spending the rest of his day watching TV.

"What a fucking joke," he said, looking at me for sympathy with eyes that were a little bit more yellow than they ought to be.

This wanker likes a drink I said to myself, wondering if we might have to carry him back to the station.

I gave him the merest of nods, and he turned his gaze to his ginger companion.

"Fuck all we can do but get on with the cunt, ey?" Wyatt replied as he pulled his tobacco pouch out of his jacket and started to hand roll a cigarette.

With such philosophical and well-spoken colleagues, it dawned on me that it really shouldn't be a surprise that there were sick bastards running around chopping people up. I have this theory that everybody, even the rich and famous and well respected, are at any time only one trigger point away from losing their shit and going on some kind of killing frenzy. Hell, I know I've felt close to that edge before, close to the point of just giving the middle finger to the world and going postal. It was easy to see how somebody could go as far as doing those things to that poor girl in the hotel room. Fearing the dark path my thoughts were taking me, I forced myself to forget it and instead took a sip of my drink. God it felt good. Bitter and smooth - exactly as advertised. That advert for those crisps popped into my head - once you pop, you can't stop – and I seriously considered the option of sacking the rest of the day off and getting smashed.

"Do you think we'll get him?"

We all looked at Perkins. All of us had at least six years on him service-wise, and you could tell. He looked uncertain and afraid, and the truth was I couldn't blame him, not after the brutality of what we'd all spent the last day and a half staring at. He waited, a half-smile on his lips. I wondered if I'd ever been so enthusiastic. I was sure I hadn't, but then again, the miserable bastard I've become probably wouldn't remember anyway. I opened my mouth to answer, but my yellow-eyed table mate, Richards, beat me to it.

"I hope so. Nobody needs someone like that out on the streets."

"Aye, cunt like that needs to be locked up wi' all the other fuckin' nutters," Wyatt added, philosophical as ever.

"I don't understand why we haven't gone public, maybe someone might have seen something?" Perkins replied.

"Trust me," I said between sips of ale. "The best thing to do now is to keep a lid on this. Letting the public in on it can do more harm than good."

"Aye. Arseholes like that love the attention. He's probably at home now, yanking on his fuckin' dick and waitin' for the news to come on." Wyatt said, gulping down a long draught.

"Jesus Wyatt," I said. "You should get a swear box or something. The rest of us could probably retire on its takings."

"Fuck off, ya cunt! I tell it how it is. Not enough people do that these days. None o' you fuckers do anyways."

Perkins nodded, looking for all the world like a conversation with Wyatt was the last thing he wanted. I was deciding between getting him off the hook by leading the chat elsewhere or drawing Wyatt into a conversation about his beloved Glasgow rangers and heaping yet more misery on Perkins, when my phone vibrated in my pocket. I fished out the overpriced (but admittedly still good) Samsung, and squinted at the display.

LUCY

1 NEW MESSAGE

I opened the text, half knowing what was to come.

ARE U OK?? YOU DIDN'T COME TO BED LAST NIGHT.

IM WORRIED ABOUT YOU. X

Half listening to Perkins and Wyatt talk about the merits of involving the public in the investigation, I punched in my reply.

ALL FINE. BUSY WITH WORK. LOT ON RIGHT NOW. X

On the Pinocchio scale, it was a whopper, and if I carried on like that, I would never become a real boy. However, sometimes, bullshit helps to keep things sweet, especially with a hormonal wife who was deep in the mood swings phase. I could have told her the truth of course – that a violent psychopath had hacked a girl to pieces not 5 miles from where we lived and put her on display to be found, and that the reason I hadn't slept was because I was sick with worry about the kind of world we intended to bring a child into, but what good would that do? It wouldn't help either her or me. And so, I fed her another lie. I wonder if there's an app for that? My phone pulsed again, and a new message popped up.

OK. LOVE YOU XXX

My thumb hovered over the touch screen as I considered my response. Of course, I love my wife, she's everything to me and the only constant in a world I feel more and more resentment towards. However I am also shit when it comes to expressing my feelings. The words just don't come, they don't feel right when they reach my throat, before they sink away again. It's always been a flaw, and although it serves me well for a cold, often disturbing, job like the one I was doing, it's pretty much catastrophic when it came to personal interactions. As usual, I went for a hazy, middle-ground shitty response, not quite committing to giving the one she was craving.

ME TOO. ILL BE HOME JUST AFTER 6. X

Martin, you complete prick. I said to myself as I pressed the send button.

Slipping the phone back into my pocket, I zoned back in on the conversation, half wishing I was alone instead of having to listen to these three numpties try to talk over each other. As was my way, I sat back and listened.

Perkins was still adamant that the public could help if we told them.

Wyatt was trying to explain how (quite rightly) it was a bad idea, and would increase our workload just from false leads alone, not that the lazy bastard ever did any work.

Richards was nodding agreement every now and again and seemed content just to sit and drink. I wondered how far gone his liver was, and decided that if you can't beat them, join them. I took a long drink, draining half my glass and becoming aware of that irritating need for nicotine as it reared its head again.

"Do you think we will catch whoever did this, Martin?"

I looked at Perkins, who was waiting for my answer, as it seemed were Wyatt and Richards.

I set my glass down and took a deep breath.

"Maybe. It depends what it is that motivates this guy. If he was just an oddball, someone who just reacted to an urge to do this on the fly then disappear into the night, then there is a good chance we won't solve this. But, if he isn't like that, if this is something he's planned and fantasised about.... if this is something he's motivated by the need to do, then I think we will have another chance to nail him."

"Why?" Perkins said, his eyes betraying the false bravado in his voice.

"Because if he went to this much trouble this time, then I would bank on him doing it again."

Nobody had any response for that, and the atmosphere at our table had changed.

"Well," I said, draining my glass. "We better get back to it, eh?"

I stood and left the three of them at the table, half hoping that this was just a one off frenzy kill. The alternative didn't bear thinking about.

* * *

Despite my assurances to Lucy, it was well after eight o'clock by the time I got home. My brain throbbed with information and exhaustion, and it dawned on me that I hadn't eaten all day. I let myself in and locked the door behind me, kicked off my shoes and hung my jacket on the pegs by the door. Lucy met me in the hallway, and just to see her gave me the lift I badly needed. She possessed that glow only pregnant women seemed to get. Her cheeks were flushed and healthy, round stomach not really taking away from her figure, but enhancing it. She'd tied her hair up into a rough ponytail. Her eyes changed when she saw me, and her greeting smile faltered a little. Maybe she could see the tension I was feeling.

"Rough day?" she asked, giving me a kiss on the cheek on the way to the kitchen.

"Yeah, sorry I'm late. Got held up in the office."

"I suspected as much. I plated you some food up if you want to microwave it."

"I'm fine, I'm not hungry." I said, even though my growling stomach disagreed.

"Did you get everything done that you needed to?"

Not exactly. You, see, we have no leads, no new information. No traceable I.D, no footage of our guy on camera. It seems he just disappeared like a phantom into the night, ready to cut up another unsuspecting prostitute, and left us scratching our arses, wondering what to do next.

"Yeah, pretty much," I said as I followed her into the kitchen, both impressed and disgusted at the ease of my lie. "How about you?"

"Midwife called in just to see how things are," she said as she waited for the kettle to boil.

"Everything okay with the baby?"

"Everything's fine," she said over her shoulder as she grabbed my 'Boss' cup from the draining board and made me a one of those awful fucking flavoured teas that she insisted on buying. Apparently they're good for relaxation, so I didn't really complain too much. I just didn't have the energy. Besides, I didn't think my preferred form of evening relaxation would go down at all well, and I tore my eyes away from the unopened bottle of Jack Daniels sitting on the counter, begging to be opened.

"Everything is going as expected, so stop worrying," she said as she handed me the cup. I winced as I turned it so I could grip the handle, and then followed her into the sitting room.

Eastenders was just finishing (one small perk of being late home was not having to sit through that dross) so I set my cup on the floor and sank onto my usual seat on the sofa. Lucy curled up next to me and just holding her close made me feel infinitely better.

"We will be okay, won't we Martin?" she said, looking up at me.

I didn't think I'd be able to do it. How could I look into those blue eyes and lie to her?

"Of course we will," I said, waiting for my nose to grow another inch or two. "We always are."

"I love you, you know. I just don't want anything to happen to you."

I stroked her hair, knowing what I should say, but as per usual, the words wouldn't come. Instead, I chose to address only the second part of what she had said.

"I'll be fine. Nothing will happen to me."

She accepted it. Maybe she was used to my inability to express myself, or maybe she just didn't see it as an issue the way I did. In any case, I was home and with the one person in the world who mattered to me. If I couldn't say it, I could definitely show her.

"How about I finish work early tomorrow and we head into town for a bite to eat?"

She sat up and grinned, and it hit me that I'd been neglecting her more than any husband had a right to.

"That would be really nice, where would you like to go?" she said, unable to stop grinning.

"Wherever you want. Your choice."

She smiled and snuggled into me, and I was grateful. Not just because I loved her, but because I knew I wouldn't be able to say it back if she said it first.

For the rest of the night, I stared at the TV without really watching. I still couldn't shake the niggling feeling in my gut that, despite what had happened so far, things were about to get much, much worse.

TUESDAY

6.

Work dragged on today. Not because I didn't enjoy it. I consider it a joy and a privilege to be allowed to gaze upon those masterpieces while mingling with people who appreciate them as much as I do. No, the reason was because I was more excited about my own hobby and where I was going with it, after a successful evening session of brainstorming. See - I know what to do now. I know how to make my mark on the world. When people are doing something impressive - or making something nice - they always say it's about quality as opposed to quantity but I disagree. It's about both. Give the people the quality they seek in whatever they're looking at but don't stop there. Hit them with both. Give them the quality and the quantity. And that's exactly what I'm going to do.

The girl in the hotel room, ignored by the press, doesn't just have to be the practice piece. I won't let her be nothing more than an experiment to encourage me to go further. She's going to be more. She's going to be the invitation that I'll be sending to the police, the media, the public. Pictures of her displayed in the hotel room are going to be the main part of the printed invitation inviting people to my gallery. A place where they can come, in their hundreds, and view the whole collection of my work in one go. Another surge of excitement rushed through me as I pictured the scene. I can see them now, coming with their cameras and notepads which would soon be filled with words praising, or damning, my work. I don't care which. Just so long as they're talking about what I've created. Just so long as they're talking about me. I'll be there too - handing out flutes of champagne from a silver tray before finally being taken away by the police for my first series of interviews. They won't catch me before then - I won't allow them to.

Having left my work place with a cheery goodbye wave to the miserable manager of the building which - I have to confess - was done more to annoy him than anything else, I jumped into my car and out of the torrential rain. The weather still mirrored yesterday's black mood. I wonder - now that I'm feeling more positive - will the sun come out? It would be nice but not ideal. The rain is good for keeping crowds of people off the streets. Instead it's just the desperate girls and boys you find walking around when it's like this. The type I want for my collection. Those no one will miss. It's easier to make them disappear without anyone else noticing in bad weather. I chuckled at the thought of what I had planned and fired up the worn-out engine before wheel-spinning from the space where I'd abandoned it that morning. No queuing for me and I'm soon on the open road heading to the one place I hate to go yet can't seem to leave behind: my old family home. The Hell-hole where I grew up with my mother and father. The perfect place to keep what needs to be stored. No one will look there, just as they didn't look for me when I needed them. They just left me there to rot and turn into what I am today. It would be the ideal hiding place and, maybe, the perfect place to put my artwork on display. After all - once out in the open - I no longer need to hide in the little flat across town pretending to be someone else. I can stand there in the middle of my work, next to my main piece, proud of what I've created and ready to answer questions posed by fans and critics.

I am here. This is who I am. Love my work. Love me.

I wasn't going to drive directly to the family home, despite wanting to get there as quickly as possible to ensure everything was just right. I wanted to swing by the hotel first. I needed to satisfy my curiosity to see if anything was happening there. I needed to see if the police had at least been called to investigate what I'd left for them. It wasn't too much of a detour anyway so it would probably only add an extra ten minutes or so onto my journey as long as the traffic wasn't bad. That's the problem when it rains - seems to make everyone turn into idiots on the road.

Imagine my relief as I saw many a police car lining the streets as I slowly drove past the hotel. It took so much effort not to stop and run in shouting to everyone that it was me who had created the masterpiece, before asking what they thought of it. I can't get carried away though. I have so much more to offer the people and, as good as it was, I didn't want to be remembered for just one piece of work - I needed a collection behind me.

I did stop though. A quick check in the rear-view mirror to see if anyone was behind me. I got out, and looked towards the hotel. I was desperate to know what was going on inside, and to find out how people were reacting to my art. Maybe I should go in and try and get a room? See if I can hear anything? I dismissed the idea just as quickly as I'd thought it. I'm still not sure as to whether they'd caught my image on a camera somewhere.

A horn suddenly beeped. I spun around. A car had pulled up behind me. I hadn't realised. Too wrapped up in what was happening in the hotel. I waved them an apology and jumped back into my own car.

I suddenly noticed a police officer watching me from the side of the road. No doubt curious as to why I slowed down to have a better look at the commotion outside of the hotel. I stamped down on the accelerator before temptation got the better of me and I found myself running up to him screaming that I was indeed the one they were looking for. A quick check of the rear-view and I saw he was still watching. Not a problem. He won't see me again. I won't be back. I saw what I needed to see. I'd confirmed that my work hadn't gone unnoticed, that it *hadn't* simply been brushed under the carpet. Next stop was the old family home to check if it really is as suitable for my plans as my imagination and memory kept telling me last night.

TUESDAY

7.

I pulled off the bumpy road and onto the gravel driveway of my parent's old home. The place where I was raised - the place where I'd spent most of my formative years wishing I was dead. My parents had died more than a few years ago through no fault of mine - not that I was sad to hear of their demise. If anything, the thought of them rotting deep in the ground brought a smile to my face; a smile broader than any other smile that I could remember. Even broader than the one I'd had on my face when finally taking a step back from my display in the hotel room to look upon it properly for the first time.

They'd left the house to me, not that I wanted it. It wasn't a move done out of love for me on their part. They'd never loved me. I'd heard that enough as I grew up; the fact that they never actually wanted me. How they'd wished I'd died within my mother's womb. A little corpse she'd gladly have expelled before displaying it within the home as a reminder to each of them to be more careful in the future. No - they didn't leave me the house as a way of showing their love or treating me well after they'd gone. They'd done it to remind me that, despite everything I do or no matter how far I run, they would always be a part of my life. They'd always be watching me from the fiery pits of Hell, hoping I fail in all that I try while laughing as my memory throws back random events from the childhood I hadn't been able to escape.

Art

I'd moved out of the house at the very first opportunity. Admittedly I'd left the shit-hole on many an occasion, but someone was always there to take me home to a mum and dad who pretended to care and acted as if they'd been concerned as to my whereabouts. As soon as the stranger had gone the beatings would continue. They couldn't keep me there forever though and, like I said, I moved out as soon as I could and very rarely returned.

I remember coming back, some years later, to pop in on them, to see how they were doing. A foolish, lonely part of me thought that perhaps they'd missed me. Perhaps my memories, distorted by time, had painted a grimmer picture than it had actually been. I knew within three minutes of stepping over the threshold that my memories had been accurate and coming home was a mistake. After that, I didn't go back until after they were dead and even then I struggled to make it much further than the hallway.

There was a part of me that wanted to sell the property as I knew I could never live there. Each room contained a different memory I'd sooner forget. Another part of me knew I couldn't get rid of it. Perhaps my subconscious had known what was coming. Perhaps the deep dark had known that I'd need a place to store my collections and props. Regardless, I was thankful the building still stood. And who knows, with what I had planned perhaps I could change negative memories into positive ones, so I could kiss goodbye the ghosts of my past once and for all. In the meantime I'm sure the negativity within these haunted walls will be more than helpful to get me in the right frame of mind to create some truly inspiring works.

I'd not been here for a couple of months, not since I'd been practising with hooks in the large shed at the back of the property. From the driveway, the house appeared to be in a good state of repair. One smashed window, God only knows why, but other than that nothing which will be too much of a challenge to fix. Good. Less time fixing things and more time to think creatively.

I fished the keys to the house out of my pocket. No sense trying to hook them outside - not in this rain. They jingled as I retrieved them. I was sure I heard my mother shouting at me to keep the noise down. Impossible, of course – she's dead. They're both dead. And I'm glad. The voices I hear aren't them. It's me, my sick mind playing tricks for reasons I've never understood. Always happens when I come back here. I just need to ignore them. I just need to keep telling myself that they're not real. And the shadow which just ran across the front window - where the lounge is - that's not real either. Just another figment of my damaged imagination. They can't hurt me now. They're gone. Keep telling myself. I shook the fears away.

I took a quick look out of the car windscreen, to see dark rain-clouds above. No sign of the downpour letting up any time soon. I'll just have to make a run for it. I braced myself for the sudden rush of winter bitterness that would hit me as soon as I opened the door. And hit me it did. Fuck, it was cold. And wet. I hurriedly got out, slammed the door and made a dash for the front entrance with the keys ready to slide straight into the lock.

It swung open and banged against the wall without too much force on my part. Wind must have caught it. The report echoed through the empty, cold house. I wished I could have kept the sound of the echo running through the deserted rooms. Normally I don't mind silence, in fact I quite enjoy it. Not in this household though. The silence here haunts me.

"Mum? Dad? You in?" I called out. I knew they weren't. I'd seen them in their boxes before they'd been dropped into the ground. I had leaned down to their still faces and had told them that I was glad they were gone. I was glad the accident had happened, and was glad the brakes had failed. But I still called their names whenever I walked into their home. Habit, I suppose. And every time I did so my heart stopped beating for a split second, long enough to realise they weren't going to answer. My heart started beating again, but skipped once more when I heard a scuttling noise going from the lounge through to the dining room. Too big to be an animal. I slammed the front door shut and hurried through to the living room. There, standing in the room adjoining the lounge, was a girl with terror etched on her face. She looked as though she hadn't washed for months. She was dressed in a tatty looking school uniform; white blouse, unbuttoned at the top and missing a tie, a gray skirt down to her knees, white socks which had slipped down her ankles. It was fair to assume she'd been a runaway for a while going by the state she was in. The dirt and general look of exhaustion on her face made it hard to determine her age. Sixteen perhaps. Maybe a year older? Homeless. The fear I'd initially felt - the fear of thinking my parents were actually still alive and that their deaths had been a figment of my imagination... but the fear disappeared as a smile crept across my lips.

"Please don't hurt me," the girl said. Was the expression on my face that transparent?

"Who are you?" I asked.

"I thought the house was empty. I watched it for a while before..."

"Ah - the window," I said, "you're what happened to the window." I took a step closer. She couldn't have moved further back. She was already standing at the furthest wall of the dining room. I'm not sure how long she had been there but it seemed pretty stupid for her to have run into a room with no exit. For her to get out now, she'd have to run straight past me and, well, that wasn't likely to happen. Under the grime caused by nights of sleeping rough and squatting where she wasn't welcome I could see that she had lovely bone structure. Her being here – I took that as a sign that my new plan was a good one, a sign that what I'm going to be doing is the right course of action.

She repeated herself again, "I thought the house was empty."

"It is," I said. Her eyes were red raw from crying. No doubt she'd been fighting her own personal demons whilst being here. Demons she probably thought would get left behind when she'd ran from wherever it was she'd come from. Despite the redness I could see that her eyes were pretty though. Very pretty. They had a sparkle about them in spite the bags and their rawness. I could only imagine what they'd have looked like had she been feeling happy. "Used to belong to my mum and dad," I told her. She looked across to the door. I could read her mind. She was wondering whether she could make it if she made a sudden run for it. I need her to relax. It will make the whole thing that much easier. I need to get to her level. "Where are your mum and dad?" I asked. She shrugged. Clearly not in a sharing mood. "I take it you have a mum and dad?" I continued. She nodded. "They'll be worried about you," I told her.

"They won't give a shit about me," she snapped. "No one will!"

I couldn't help but smile. Music to my ears. The poor little girl who nobody wanted.

Well she's in luck.

I want her.

"You can stay here if you want. For the time-being at least." I told her. "I own a place on the other side of the town. Not sure what I want to do with this place yet. Bad memories." It didn't hurt her knowing the truth. She wouldn't be around for long. Certainly not long enough to tell anyone anyway - not by the time she realises who

I really am. "I just come by here, from time to time, to make sure the place is okay. You staying here for now - well that would just do me a favour. Means you can keep an eye on the place..." At least until I'm more prepared and come back to take out those pretty little eyes. Ideas were already formulating in the back of my mind, hidden from her, as to what I would do to her little teenage body. The eyes would be taken out, and the skin cut from her bones to be sewn back together to make up a fleshy duvet to keep her bony body warm at night. She'll make a great display; the sulky teenage girl locked away in one of the bedrooms upstairs - hiding under the duvet from the monsters under the bed. Obviously that's just the first idea that popped in my mind. I have time to work on it. Make it really spectacular. Give her a scenario of which she'd be proud.

"You're not going to phone the police?" she asked.

"Phone the police? Why would I do that?"

"I broke a window," she confessed.

"No you didn't," I flashed her my most sincere smile once more, "a branch did that..."

For the first time since seeing me standing in the house, she smiled back at me.

"You make yourself at home. I take it you have no money? You have no food?"

She shook her head, "No."

"Well leave that to me. I'll go to the shops in the local village and get some bits in for you. How's that sound?" I asked.

"Why are you being so nice to me?"

"The world's a shitty place," I told her, "and sometimes it's nice to do something for someone else." She had no idea that she'd be the one doing something for me. In time - she'd be the one doing *me* the favour. My act of kindness was nothing more than taking an opportunity to buy her life. She has a roof, she'll have food and so she'll have no reason to go anywhere. And then - when she wants to leave – it'll be too late. She will be my second work of art.

WEDNESDAY

8.

It was shaping up to be another frustrating day when we finally got a lucky break. One of those pretend police, or community officers as they go by these days, had only just decided to tell us that he saw a guy drive past the hotel on Tuesday night, acting oddly. Why the hell they didn't think it was worth reporting straight away I don't know, but either way, it's a lead, which is more than we had this morning. We even managed to get a registration for the car. More good luck. As much as I was glad to get a break, it was almost lunchtime, which meant my half day's holiday was about to kick in. I stood up and grabbed my coat.

"Where are you goin, ya cunt?" The ever eloquent Wyatt said as I shut my PC off.

"Early finish,"

"Alright for some eh?"

"I still do more work in half a day than you manage in a week, Wyatt," I shot back, tipping him a wink.

"What do you want me to do about this lead with the car?" Perkins said as I crossed the room.

"Trace the owner, see what you can dig up. Tomorrow you can come with me and we'll go ask him what he was doing at the scene."

Perkins nodded. I could have waited around for the trace results and gone that afternoon of course but that would have meant staying in the office, which would have meant I would have probably ended up working late and missing my night out with Lucy, and God knows, a bit of time together is something we both desperately needed. It wasn't lost on me that I had become a miserable old bastard over the last few weeks, and I was eager to make it up to her. Ignoring the crude jibes of the ginger warrior I left my colleagues at the station behind and headed for home.

* * *

Lucy and I had always shared a great, natural understanding. An effortless ability to be comfortable around each other right from the moment we met, which only made the awkward silence and forced conversation both difficult and hard to understand as we made our way through our evening. For something that was supposed to be a good way for us to spend some time together, it was rapidly becoming a torturously slow evening, or as my pal Wyatt might have said, a fuckin' cuntin' clusterfuck of a date night.

I pushed potatoes and overpriced fish around my plate as I tried to think of something to say that wasn't a lie and which didn't rely on me being open with my feelings. Actually, thinking about it, it's no surprise I was struggling to make conversation. I looked at Lucy, and winced inside. She had really made an effort. Her hair was straightened and styled to half cover one eye, and she was wearing an expensive black dress. She smiled, but I only saw pity and concern, and I suddenly hated myself even more.

"How was work?" she asked, seemingly content to avoid the emotional minefield for the time being.

"Not bad," I said, hoping that I wouldn't have to go Pinocchio on her again.

"Are you sure? You seem really....distant lately."

Here it comes.

To avoid having to immediately answer, I put a forkful of that expensive fish in my mouth and chewed slowly, giving me time to think of something to say that was at least a little bit honest.

"I suppose I'm feeling the stress a little lately."

Well done Martin. That was almost the truth. Jiminy Cricket would be proud.

"You shouldn't work yourself so hard. I worry about you."

I worry about the world that our baby will have to live in.

The words almost made it out, but as usual they got stuck in my throat, and I swallowed them back down with a sip of the (also overpriced) wine.

"I'm fine, really," I said, even managing a genuine smile. Someone give me a best actor Oscar. "We just have a couple of big cases on right now and we're stretched a little thin. Anyway, we didn't come here to talk about work. Let's just enjoy each other's company."

Art

"Do you still love me?"

Uh oh.

I couldn't chew my way around this one. It was a direct question, and she was staring at me, waiting for an answer. I knew that the longer I delayed, the worse it would sound, but my stupid tongue refused to move from the bottom of my stupid mouth. With what amounted to a tremendous force of will, I blurted out my stupid answer.

"Why would you even ask that?"

It wasn't great, but it was the best I could do.

"You never say it, you barely show it. I sometimes wonder if having the baby has frightened you off." Her lip trembled and she broke eye contact. I knew she would never cry, especially out in public, but she couldn't quite hide the hurt, and that made me feel like an even bigger bastard than I did already. Without realising I was going to do it, I reached across the table and took her hands in mine.

"You and the baby are the best thing that ever happened to me. Don't ever think otherwise."

Alright. That wasn't bad.

"Why can't you say it? Why can't you tell me you love me?"

"I do."

"Then say it. Say the words."

I

LOVE

YOU

Come on tongue. Just three little words. Hell, one of them isn't even a word. It's just a letter. You can skip out on the 'I' If you want, just say the other two words, pleaaase, you're making me look bad here.

Ever stubborn, my tongue stayed where it was.

Bastard thing.

"Don't be silly," I said, managing three words even if they weren't the ones I wanted to say. "I shouldn't have to prove this to you. We've been together for so long, been through so much together. Surely that proves enough how I feel about you."

"But why can't you say it?"

She was getting frustrated now, and I was too. People were starting to glance over at us from neighbouring tables. I lowered my voice as I replied to her.

"I... I struggle sometimes to express my emotions, that's all. It's hard for me."

"Even to me?"

"To anyone. There are things going on that you don't know and..."

I had said too much. I was hoping she would miss it, but I was only fooling myself. She was a woman after all, and in my experience, they don't miss anything.

"Things I don't know? Are you seeing someone else?"

"Good god, no," I said, even managing to laugh. It was the first genuine emotion I had felt for a long time, and it worried me that it felt more alien than the lies I had begun to surround myself in. "Absolutely not. I can't believe you could even ask me that."

She nodded, "I'm sorry, I just had to ask. You understand that don't you?"

"I get why you asked, but you absolutely don't have to worry about that. I promise you, I swear on our baby's life. I would never be unfaithful to you."

She believed me, and so she should. It was the absolute truth. Unfortunately, that conversation killed the rest of the night. We barely spoke as we finished our meal, then ate our desserts and had coffee.

There was a sense of irony that both of us were just going through the motions, desperate to get out of that restaurant and back home so we could at least stop pretending to be part of the upper classes. I got so desperate to leave that I barely flinched at the bill, which I think cost more than the GDP of some small countries. I just wanted to pay and get out of there. Neither of us spoke much when we got home. Lucy went straight to bed, I sat up for a while and felt sorry for myself, which was something I was getting good at. I really,

really wanted to go buy some cigarettes, and even though I almost caved, I settled for a hot shower and early night instead.

What a mess.

I climbed into bed, trying not to disturb Lucy, but she turned to face me and put her head on my chest.

"I just want to feel like you love me," she whispered in her half-asleep murmur.

Surely now, when it was just us in the privacy of our own room, I could say it.

"Will you say it if I'm nice to you?" she whispered, reaching below the sheets and taking me in hand.

As much as it was an unexpected turn of events, it seemed even my loins were ashamed of me, and like my tongue, decided to play dead.

"It's late, we should get some sleep," I said as I pushed her hand away and turned onto my side.

You bastard. You absolute bastard.

I wished for the bed to open up and swallow me down to the kind of hellish torture I surely deserved. As I lay there on my side, I had to listen to my rejected wife cry herself to sleep. The only thing I could think about, was how much I really, really needed a cigarette.

WEDNESDAY

9.

I can't remember the last time I phoned in sick to work. It's not something that I tend to do. For some reason - given the way I am - I hate letting people down when I'm supposed to do something. Maybe that's why I don't want to let them down with my artwork. I want to give them something special - just like my father wanted to touch the world with his brush strokes. I know I'm a monster, my soul somewhat tainted by a comfortable darkness, but at least I'm a monster with morals. These people - at work - counted on me to do a job and I didn't want to let them down. I didn't want to leave them short-staffed. Didn't have a choice though. I wanted to make sure the girl was okay. I wanted to make sure she was comfortable in my old family home. I snorted. Who would have thought someone would have finally been able to find some comfort within those walls. Certainly not me.

"Must have eaten something yesterday," I'd told Gary when he finally came to the phone. He was fine when I told him. No doubt because I rarely did things like this. Made it seem that little more believable as opposed to someone who constantly called in. He just wished me well - a speedy recovery - and asked whether I thought I'd be in on the Thursday. I would be in tomorrow but I didn't tell him that. I just said that I hoped to be. I figured if you were that ill - with a sickness bug - and you felt the need to phone in and tell them you weren't going in then you probably wouldn't know for certain whether you'd be better the next day. "Certainly hope so," I'd said, "already bored of daytime television!" Gary laughed and told me to rest up before letting me get back to what he thought to be my bed. Little did he know. When I called him, I was talking on my mobile phone sitting in my car - parked up at a supermarket close to the other side of town. Not the usual shop I went to, because I didn't want to risk bumping into anyone from work given the circumstances.

With the call finished I calmly slid the phone into my jacket pocket and stepped out of the car - more rain - before I ran towards the supermarket's entrance, taking a hold of a basket as I walked in. Let's get this done. Keep her happy. Make her feel secure.

* * *

A couple of hours later, I was back at the family home. I let myself in, and saw the young lady standing at the far end of the hallway. The same nervous look on her face as I'd seen yesterday. I smiled at her, but not because I was trying to put her at ease. I did so because she hadn't disappeared in the night; run off to somewhere else to hole up. Another sign that this is meant to be. A gift from God.

"Still here?" I said. She didn't say anything, instead she just awkwardly shifted her feet. "That's good." I stayed where I was - I needed to win her trust to make things easier when the time came. Didn't want to have to chase her after all. Not that she'd get far. I know this house, and the surrounding woods, like the back of my hand. There's no way she'd get away. Even so - I wanted to keep things simple. "I wasn't sure what you liked so I picked up... well... a fair amount actually. I mean there isn't any gas, electric or even water here so must of it is things like crisps and biscuits and bread - you know - bits and pieces which might last a little longer..." I held up the bags to prove what I was saying was true.

"Why are you doing this?" she asked. Funny but I thought we had cleared this up yesterday. "What do you want?"

"What do I want? Nothing," I lied. "You're doing me a favour by staying here. I explained yesterday. And like I said - you can stay for as long as you need to. It gives me time to decide what to do with the place. You know, whether to sell it or whether to maybe move back in."

There was a slight pause. One which was long enough for me to wonder whether I'd ever win her trust or whether I'd be better off just disposing of her now before she became a liability. "Do you need a hand?" she asked. I smiled. Perhaps winning her trust wouldn't be as hard as I'd thought.

"Would be nice," I said, picking up two of the bags. She came down the hallway then and straight past me, stepping from the house to fetch more shopping from the car. More surprisingly - and for the first time ever - I realised that I had entered the house without acknowledging the ghosts of my parents. I guess she really is doing me a favour by staying here. Already I feel more comfortable.

By the time the bags had all been brought in she seemed to be comfortable enough to stand close to me. At times she even stood close by with her back to me; a sure sign of trust if ever I needed one.

The two of us were standing in the kitchen - emptying the shopping onto the work surfaces.

"How old are you?" I asked suddenly. I wasn't able to ignore the fact she looked so young. Too young, for sure, to be on the streets as a runaway.

"I'm seventeen," she said, "nearly eighteen."

I nodded, "Just - with the school uniform... I thought you might be younger," I told her. I felt relieved that she was of age. Had she said she were sixteen - or younger - I might have had to release her. I'm not entirely sure why I couldn't have gone through with what needed to be done (if she were under the age of consent). I guess I have some morals after all? Not a complete monster. I guess I want her to be remembered as a piece of my artwork as opposed to 'just another murdered' child.

She explained the uniform, "I went to a posh school. You have a choice of continuing to study with them if your grades are good enough. You know - after you've got your GCSE marks through." She went quiet. "My grades were the only decent thing about my life." The pair of us fell into an awkward silence once more.

I extended my hand towards her. "My name's Ian," I lied. If you'd asked me why I had thought it necessary to lie to her, I couldn't have told you. I guess I'd just grown used to calling myself by different names and Ian happened to be the name on the credit card I'd bought the shopping with. I guess my mind is trying to keep me in character incase people ever talk to me at a checkout. They might question as to why the name I gave was different to the one on the card I was handing over. Not that I've ever been in a position where that even had the slightest possibility of happening. I guess I just like to be prepared. God knows I'd spent enough time making sure as to not leave prints at the hotel. Would be stupid to get caught out now just because I was discovered using fake identification and credit cards.

To my surprise the girl shook my hand. "I'm Mandy," she said.

"Well - I'm not sure what brought you to my house and it's none of my business, but I'm pleased to meet you," I said. I didn't care about the details of her life - I was just happy that she was here. A true stroke of luck.

I emptied the last bag, a handful of candles which she could use to keep the place illuminated whilst we waited for the electricity, gas and water to come back on - something, I'm assured by the utility companies, which will happen within twenty-four hours.

I scrunched the empty bag into a small ball. "Hopefully there are some bits here that you like," I told her as I took a step back from her. It was one thing being polite and trying to win her trust. It was another thing entirely to want to stay in close proximity. I am, after all, someone who grew up treasuring my own space. She didn't answer. She just stared at me. A look in her eyes that I didn't recognise. Without any warning she started to unbutton her white blouse. "What are you doing?" I asked.

She opened her blouse and revealed the cotton bra underneath.

"Isn't this what you want?"

I put my hand out and stopped her from stripping any further. At first I wasn't sure that was what I wanted, whether I was going to stop her or touch her. Fuck her. Be inside her. Taste her cunt whilst it was still warm and alive. I was a little disappointed to find myself stopping her but I guess that's what my subconscious wanted.

"That's not what I want." I reassured her. I'll take her life, but I won't take her obvious innocence. She started to cry and, before I knew it, I found myself wrapping my arms around her and holding her tight. She was shaking. "It's okay," I told her. "Everything is okay." My lying is pure master-class and my mask is getting some good use today.

I can only imagine the shock on her face when I do finally get around to squeezing the life out of her.

* * *

I left the girl to prepare some sandwiches whilst I took a look around the rest of the house, having told her that I just wanted to make sure everything else was still structurally sound. Three bedrooms upstairs and a bathroom, a lounge/dining room downstairs along with a small study, toilet and kitchen. It was a fair sized property - definitely more than enough space for what I wanted it for - and could have been a nice place to raise a family if it weren't for the bad memories. Just as I had initially thought about the hotel though - I can't help but wonder whether people would sooner this house be pulled to the ground by the time I'm finished with it.

"I don't understand why you don't live here." Mandy's voice, from behind me, made me jump. I turned to see her standing in the doorway with two paper plates - which I had purchased along with the food - in her hands. "It's a nice home," she continued as she handed me one of the plates. I took it and sat myself on a dusty sofa. She sat next to me, making me feel a little like my personal space was being invaded, and took a bite out of her sandwich before continuing, "I mean it could do with a lick of paint here and there but - I'd like to live here," she said.

"We're all running away from something." I didn't want to go into the details. It wasn't necessary. Just as she didn't want to go into why she had run away from home. Me and her - we were both running away. The only difference was that I was still running long after my parents had died whilst hers were alive. She took another bite from her sandwich. The way she was chewing - I'm guessing she hadn't eaten for a while. Probably half starved. Good. Means she'll struggle less when the time comes. I'll just have to make sure I kill her before she gets all of her strength back. Although, looking at her, it won't be that much of an issue if I do have to take her on at her best. I'll still snap her like a twig.

"What are you running away from?" I asked her. I knew she wouldn't answer but I was keen to turn the conversation away from myself. I didn't want to think about my parents - my mother who turned to alcohol to hide from my father's violent mood swings. My father, an artist who'd spend his days and evenings painting away at his work which people would then just label as being of 'poor quality' before dismissing him completely. A failure in his chosen field.

He blamed me for taking away his creativity. Having to look after a son - whilst mum went out to work - took too much time and energy. Apparently killed his creative flow and passion. Before I was born his work sold. After I came along - no one wanted it anymore. And then mother - she'd come home from work drunk - she'd put the blame for the failing marriage and the way dad treated her solely at my feet too. Neither of them wanted me around. Neither of – shit! Stop thinking about it! I tried to dismiss the thoughts but struggled as their voices echoed through my head.

We didn't want you, you know. You'll amount to nothing. You know that don't you? You're nothing but a waste of space. What anyone could ever see in you is beyond us. We didn't want you, you know. You'll amount to nothing. You know that don't you? You're nothing but a waste of space. What anyone could ever see in you is beyond us. We didn't want you, you know. You'll amount to nothing. You know that don't you? You're nothing but a waste of space. What anyone could ever see in you is beyond us. We didn't want you, you know. You'll amount to nothing. You know that don't you? You're nothing but a waste of space. What anyone could ever see in you is beyond us... STOP IT!

Mandy's voice distracted me from the poisoned thoughts, "My dad," she said, her voice shaky, "he'd come to my room at night." I could already see where this was going. Everything became clear to me; the reason why a girl so young had offered herself so freely to me because she thought it was what I wanted.

"I get it," I told her. We were even in regards to favours now. She was doing me a favour looking after the house whilst I made plans around her. She was also doing me the favour of being the second piece of artwork for my collection. In turn, I was giving her shelter - somewhere safe to stay and then, when the time was right, I was going to ensure her father could never hurt her again by taking her from the world he foolishly brought her into. I smiled at her, as sympathetically as I could muster. It must have worked because she returned it. I wanted to tell her not to worry and that - before she knew it - everything would be over with but I didn't want to frighten the girl. Not yet. "I best be getting back to my flat," I said as I suddenly stood up.

"You haven't finished your sandwich!" she pointed out. She was right. I hadn't finished it but I wasn't hungry. I had done what I needed to do. There was no point in staying. "Can't you stay a while longer?" she asked. I shook my head. Don't want to get emotionally attached to her. Not that there was much danger of that.

"Sorry - I have things to do." Like, people to kill. It's a busy life.

"But you'll come back?" she asked. She sounded desperate, as though she yearned for my company. I wonder if she'd be as enthusiastic for me to stay if she knew who I really was and what I was capable of. I doubt it somehow.

"You'll see me soon enough," I told her. She smiled. Something tells me she won't be as happy to see me the next time I come on by.

THURSDAY

10.

"Is it safe to come in here?" Gary asked from the locker room doorway. Our daily meet-and-greet before the start of our shift. I caught sight of his reflection in the small mirror, attached to the inside of the locker door. He had his hand over his mouth as though worried there was a chance he could catch some germs from me.

"Pretty sure you're safe," I told him. Unless of course I wanted to use him as a display piece in which case he most definitely wouldn't be safe. I flushed the unexpected dark thought from my mind as I pinned my name badge on. The metaphorical mask I wore for the world at large slipped back into place. "I'm sorry about yesterday," I said. Even I was surprised at how sincere I sounded. Perhaps I really *was* sorry. Could it be that I was actually feeling guilty about having pulled a sickie? I tried not to laugh. Of all the things to feel guilty about - it's something as mundane as pulling a sickie. Don't laugh. Especially not now, after having just apologised for not coming to work yesterday.

"These things happen," said Gary. He walked into the room and removed his hand from his mouth. "Something you ate, huh?"

As per usual I placed my wallet and keys on the small shelf in the little cupboard. "Must have been."

"Nasty. See - I'm lucky. Years of eating my wife's cooking and my stomach is like cast iron. So used to the crap that nothing catches it by surprise anymore." He suddenly stopped and turned to me. Was that a joke? Was I supposed to laugh or tell him how funny he was? I said nothing. "You might as well hear it from me," he said, "the powers that be had a talk with me on Monday. I was going to talk to you yesterday but, obviously that proved impossible when you didn't come in. Unfortunately they're making cut backs and, well, I'm one of those cut backs. They've given me until the end of the month. Probably because of my age, I guess, not that they'll ever admit it."

"I'm sorry to hear that." I said. What do you know? I actually am sorry to hear that. Could it be that, since getting a piece of my art out of my system I'm becoming more human with each passing day? First of all I help out a homeless girl - admittedly I thought I was doing it for other reasons - and then I feel guilty about calling in sick and now I'm here actually feeling sorry that Gary is leaving. He's a good bloke.

"Yeah. I'll miss this place," he said. From the expression on his face, the fact he looked as though he was going to weep, I could tell he was being genuine. I guess I'd feel the same if the shoe was on the other foot and it was me getting my marching orders. The thought of not coming here - not being able to see the art on a daily basis and mingle with the folk who enjoy looking at it... "Listen, before I go, you're going to have to come over to mine for a meal with the wife," he said. His voice was suddenly upbeat. He almost sounded positive. Was he wearing a mask too? "How does that sound?" he asked when I didn't answer.

"Er - sure." Of course I wouldn't go but I wasn't about to tell him that. Seemed cruel. Suddenly a mental image flashed up in my mind; he was sitting opposite his wife. Both of them were dead. Their faces submerged in bowls of soup. The sound of flies coming from speakers hidden under the table. A little plague that read 'The Last Supper' being the centre piece of the scene. I smiled. Guess I'm not becoming more human after all.

"Tell you what - I'll even make sure we get a takeaway," he continued, "we don't need the wife giving you another round of food poisoning!" he laughed. "Mind you," his voice changed to a darker tone, "if you're that ill - I guess I could always cover your shifts... you know - until you're feeling better! If you get better that is..." The sudden change in his character surprised me. Just another example of a darkness within our surroundings that we're not used to seeing or hearing. It's always there though, bubbling away under the surface. He laughed. I laughed too out of politeness. "Sound like a plan?" he asked.

"You covering my shifts whilst I recover from being poisoned by your wife?"

"The takeaway. Want to make a date of it?" he looked hopeful for me to say yes. My lacking social skills couldn't determine whether he was genuinely wanting me to go round for dinner or whether he was just being polite. Best keep it positive but non-committal.

"It sounds nice. I'd like that. Let me check my diary when I get home tonight and I'll come back to you with when I'm free. See if we can work something out," I said. I didn't keep a diary at home. I only said it because I hoped he'd forget by tomorrow or that neither of us would mention it again.

"You do that," said Gary. "I'll warn my wife." He smiled at me as he turned his attention back to his locker while I closed mine. "You never know, we might be lucky and she might decide to leave us to it, and go round her sister's for the night."

I laughed, again unsure of whether he was being genuine. Did he really hate his wife that much? When I see people like this, people like my own mother and father and the relationship they had together, sometimes I'm glad I'm different. Sometimes I think the way I am is easier than the way these people need to behave. I wear one mask and that's for when I'm with anyone other than myself and my victims. When I'm alone, or when I was with that whore in the hotel room, I was just me being me. Gary, though... how many masks does he have? He has a mask for when he's with strangers - he becomes a seemingly polite man there to lend a helping hand - he has a mask for when he is with his wife - the man who loves her dearly - and then, when he is with his friends, he becomes plain old Gary. My way is definitely easier.

* * *

I hardly looked at any of the exhibits as I walked around the gallery. My mind couldn't focus. Instead I was more concerned with the people coming into the building. The ones who'd idly walk into my area, completely unaware of me watching them, in their own little worlds as they gazed upon the masterpieces. With each new person, my mind quickly judged as to whether they should carry on with their meaningless life or whether they deserved to become a part of my own collection. A pointless exercise as I wouldn't touch any of them. The kind of people who come to places like this tend to be families or school trips. Either group would be missed if they suddenly disappeared. Not like the whore. No one would miss a whore. Or a homeless person. Or a runaway like the girl currently resting in my home. This - what I am doing with the people visiting the gallery - this is just practice. This is just getting my brain used to not worrying about hurting the people that I choose to take in the name of art. Not that I've ever really had that problem before. I just need to be sure that there really is no chance of me becoming more human over the course of time. The last thing I need is to grow a conscience when I have a house full of guests. Not that I think that would really be an issue, certainly not after what I did to the whore. If I was going to start having qualms - if I wasn't going to be able to complete the task, I would have folded then.

My mind drifted back to the hotel room. I was pacing the room, backwards and forwards, waiting for that faint knock on the wooden door to signal that my date had arrived. For a short period, as the time grew closer, I contemplated not answering. I thought I could just ignore her and she'd go away. Perhaps she might mouth off through the door, or call me all the names under the sun but she would have lived on to fuck another day and I'd have not become what I am today.

I'd have been as normal as my damaged upbringing allowed for. When the knock did finally come, a couple of minutes later than scheduled, all thoughts of ignoring it disappeared and I didn't hesitate in opening the door, a nervous smile of apprehension on my face.

"Hi I'm Naomi!" she'd said. She stood there in a tight fitting dress, and looked amazing considering she was from one of the less-expensive escort agencies. When I'd originally booked her I didn't think I'd have sex with her, because that isn't really my thing. I usually found that I struggled to achieve the orgasm that people crave when indulging in sexual activities. Sure, I got there in the end but only because I was thinking about the art I wanted to create. If I'd thought about the person I was with, or even just the sensations I felt, well - it would take me forever to finish and I found that I soon got bored. This girl was different, the one standing in front of me at the hotel room. I'm not sure whether it's because I thought she was pretty or because I knew what I was going to do to her but I knew I'd fuck her.

Standing in the corner of my room within the larger gallery, I shifted uneasily as I became aware of my growing erection. The thoughts of judging who could be a part of my work and the thought of fucking that whore whilst throttling the life out of her - knowing what I'd be doing to her still-warm corpse when I finished - clearly excited me. I held my hands in front of my crotch to hide from any further embarrassment as I suppressed my smile. Don't need to attract more attention to myself than necessary.

I dig your shirt, I heard Naomi's voice in my head. I tried to shake it away but I couldn't. I just stood there, in the corner, grinning like an idiot in spite of my best efforts. I remembered how her hand had stroked my chest. I remembered, at the time, how I had felt my cock grow at her touch and how I feverishly handed her the money. She had asked me what my name was. I can't remember the one I gave her, I've used so many now. She had asked me what I was doing in town. I concocted some story about being on a business seminar. I changed the subject back to her just to stop from having to over complicate things with more lies. She invited me to sit with her on the corner of the bed - an invitation I accepted when she pulled me across the mattress. We sat down together as she told me she thought I was cute before kissing me - her tongue sliding seductively into my mouth. Unexpected but appreciated. Before I knew what was happening my hands were on her sides as her own hands were rubbing my crotch.

I left my post and hurriedly headed towards the toilet. Need to calm myself down. Need to get this out of my system before someone sees what I'm pitching or that I'm acting strangely.

The toilet was just down the corridor thankfully, so not far to go. I ran into the far cubicle and locked the door, my memory playing back what had happened in the hotel room.

You're cute! She'd told me before instructing me to take my clothes off. An order I'd complied with as she slipped out of her own tight dress to reveal her matching underwear set.

I couldn't help but unbutton my trousers and free my pulsing erection. The feeling of it being free was infinitely more comfortable than having it trapped within my tight work trousers, all squashed up and nowhere to go. This isn't what I usually do. This isn't what I like. Yet I couldn't help but wrap my hand around it and start stroking it as my mind continued to tease me with thoughts of the hotel room and dear Naomi. The feeling of being inside of her. Despite the condom, I felt everything. I remembered how tight she'd felt. I remembered how surprised I was at the discovery. I remember thinking that I presumed she'd have been a little on the loose side given the day job and amount of cock she sees. More importantly I remembered how fucking *good* it had felt.

I quickened my stroke. She *had* felt good. And the lustful look on her face, as she'd played the part of the ultimate girlfriend experience, had been a sight to behold. But I'd preferred how she'd looked next - her eyes bulging as I strangled her. The panic-stricken look, skin red-flushed as I pressed on her neck harder. I remember thinking I was sure I'd felt my penis harden that little bit more. A twitch from it. The thought of what I did to that girl was more exciting than the thought of fucking her. Or perhaps it was the combination of the two - being inside her as she died. I came as she went. I stroked harder and faster as I remembered the orgasm - clearly the best orgasm I had ever experienced – while I'd stared directly into her dying eyes and heard the last of her breath escape her body. And just as I had ejaculated then, another hard orgasm hit and I ejaculated over the toilet cubicle. Out of breath but immediately relaxed, I couldn't help myself when a little laugh escaped my lips. First time for everything I guess. I only hoped that the toilet was empty. Didn't want to bump into anyone as I left - especially if they'd heard what I'd been doing, which I'm sure they would have done...

* * *

The rest of the afternoon went by without incident, once I'd managed to calm myself down. I still couldn't believe I'd done it, even as I drove home. More to the point, I couldn't believe how good it had felt. As I've said, that's not me. I don't do that. It never really does anything for me but that - that was something special. After that I saw why people masturbated. Put me down as a convert!

I entered my apartment building and took the stairs to the third floor, where my domicile was. I could have used the lift to save on energy after the long day of standing on my feet but it takes forever and, even if it was the fastest lift in the world, it always stank of urine despite the rest of the place being in a fair condition. It always baffled me as to why the lift always smelled so bad. It was as if a homeless person staggered in late at night, drunk on rot-gut alcohol, taken a piss in it and then disappear again. Maintenance had been told of the smell on numerous occasions, not by me but by others who'd even taken it upon themselves to go door to door to talk to the other residents about it. Thankfully I'd seen them as they approached and had realised what they were doing so - when they came knocking for me, I simply didn't answer.

A little out of breath when I got to my floor, I turned down the corridor and froze when I spotted two men standing outside my door. They looked official to say the least in their cheap looking suits - no doubt purchased from some budget catalogue which afforded them the luxury of paying in instalments. I took a deep breath, suppressed any feelings of unease at their presence, got back into character, and approached with caution.

"Can I help you at all?" I asked, as I neared the two of them.

One of them flashed a badge at me. I didn't get a good look at it but saw enough to know it was an official piece of police identification. My heart skipped a beat - not that I let it show. Stupid really. Nothing to panic about. Other than the hotel room escapades, I hadn't done anything. Unless feeding a homeless girl is against the law now and no one had told me. So why are they here? It can't be because of what I'd done in the hotel room. I'd been careful to cover my tracks, and the card I'd used to purchase the products for my masterpiece - well that particular one had never been linked to this address.

"Damon Benton?" one of them asked. I nodded. "My name is Detective Inspector Andrews, this is my colleague, Constable Perkins. We are conducting enquiries about a recent incident and wondered if we might have a word?

"Oh? Well, you'd better come in then," I replied. Keep calm. Don't show you're nervous. Don't give him anything. It's probably just routine. They have nothing on you. They couldn't have anything.

You were careful, *super* careful. I slid my front door key into the lock and twisted it. It clicked across and allowed me to push the door open. I stepped in first before holding it open for the two officers. I closed it again after them. "So what can I do for you?" I asked.

"Are you the owner of a light blue Renault Espace, registration HV06 GUC?"

I nodded. "That's my car." Two police officers sent over because I had been caught speeding perhaps? No. That's silly. They'd have just posted through a letter inviting me to attend court or simply fined me and told me to send off my documents to receive the necessary penalty points. "Is there a problem?"

"What were you doing at the Faircrest Hotel on Tuesday evening? Witnesses place you at the location a little after… What time was it Perkins?"

"6pm, sir."

"A little after 6pm. Would you like to tell us why you were there?"

This is all because I went back to the hotel? I cast my mind back - a look on my face suggesting to the officer that I was trying to remember what I had been doing - and remembered the man in the police uniform watching my car. Watching me get out of it, then get back in and drive away. "Yes," I told him the truth. "I remember it because of all the police cars parked outside it. I wondered what had gone on to cause a need for so many officers. Whatever it was - must have been bad although, having said that, it couldn't have been too bad because I didn't see anything on the news about it. Nor did I read anything in the papers the next day if memory serves correctly. What happened?"

I knew they wouldn't tell me but it just seemed an obvious thing for an innocent person to ask, especially having been confronted by two officers. The second officer made a note in his pad. I couldn't tell what he was writing but was curious to know. Nothing I had said could have been perceived as noteworthy - surely. "I was thinking about booking a room there," I told them. "Thought it looked like a nice place to take this lady I'm seeing..."

"You wouldn't bring her back here?"

"Would you? Have you been in the lift?" I asked with a smile, knowing full well that they wouldn't have used the stairs. Neither officer returned my smile. If anything I think it made them scowl that little bit more. Come on mask. Work your magic. Make me appear normal. Make me appear innocent. "Anyway, the sight of all the police cars put me off." The second officer was still scribbling notes down in his pad. "Just as well really," I continued, "lady friend dumped me anyway," I said, painting myself as a tragic figure as opposed to potential killer and psychopath.

"I think that just about covers everything for now. If you think of anything that may be of interest, don't hesitate to call. We might well be back to speak to you again."

I took the card from his hand and looked at the name. Detective Martin Andrews. A phone number. Some other information. Hardly the most inspiring card but then I guess they don't really get a say in how their card looks. Still, at least it let me know who was working my case. Our little meeting was unproductive for him but, for me it opened the door to really have some fun. Something to pass the time until my gallery was ready for the grand unveiling. Have to be careful though in case they get too close.

I showed them to the door and watched as they walked down the corridor. Little does he know, he's just sealed the fate of poor little Mandy. I smiled as I closed the door before sliding the business card into my pocket. Interesting.

* * *

"So what do you think?" Perkins asked as we walked back down to the car.

"I'm not sure yet, he seemed straight enough. He was forthcoming about his answers at any rate." Perkins nodded, and I could tell he had something on his mind.

"Spit it out, what are you thinking?"

We clambered into the car, and I fired up the engine, warming my hands on the heater.

"I don't know, he seemed a little… off to me."

"In what way?"

"I don't know, I can't explain it."

"Could be that you're looking for things that aren't there. We've all done that, especially when we're just starting out. Try not to make personal judgements. Let the evidence do that for you. If he's guilty, then something will come up we can use to nail him. Until then, best if we just let this play out."

"I hope it does," Perkins said as I put the car into gear and headed back towards the station. "It's the only lead we have."

There was no answer to that, so I chose not to reply. Instead we drove in silence. As far as weeks went, this one couldn't end soon enough.

FRIDAY

11.

"What's this?" I asked as I eyed the box on my desk.

"Came for you this morning," Perkins said without looking up from his computer.

"You sure it's for me?"

"It's got your name on it hasn't it, ya dopey cunt!" Wyatt said with his usual charm and grace.

I eyed up the package and saw that it did indeed have my name carefully printed on the label. I wondered if it was from Lucy, another apology that she neither owed me nor that I deserved. We had barely spoken at all since the farce at the meal, and the last couple of days had been spent with me mostly walking on eggshells and trying not to make things worse. There was no disguising it though. The gulf between us was growing wider.

"Maybe you have a secret admirer eh, Martin?" Wyatt said, flashing his yellowed, gap-toothed grin. As much as I liked to join in with the banter, I really couldn't be arsed, so I let it slide and turned my attention back to the box. The rest of my mail I set aside. It was the usual forests worth of shite. Copies of reports or witness statements, other stuff that would just get shoved into a drawer for a year until it was thrown out unread. The day these bastards go paperless will be a day for celebration. My phone buzzed in my jacket, and I snatched it out, hoping it would be Lucy, but it was another one of those fucking spam mails about reclaiming PPI charges. Those bastards ought to get a real job instead of cluttering up the inboxes of people who didn't give a shit about the services they offered. With my day going from bad to worse, I shoved the phone back into my pocket and peeled the tape off the box. And looked inside.

There was another smaller box inside. It looked like a shoebox. I pulled off the lid, and it took me a few seconds to register what I was seeing. I lurched away from my desk, sending my chair rolling across the floor and crashing into the filing cabinet.

"What is it," Wyatt asked as he got up and came towards me, as did everyone else in the office.

I was numb. I couldn't move, I didn't know what to do.

"Someone get fuckin' forensics in here, now!" Wyatt shouted.

"Are you okay Martin?"

I think it was Perkins, but he sounded as if he were underwater. Either way I was in no fit state to answer him. All I could do was stare into the box.

The note said just two simple words. 'See Me' scrawled in marker pen. One corner was stained with blood. Around it, mounted on sticks were two eyes, their bulbous mass still fleshy with optical nerves hanging like macabre decorations. My stomach rolled, then tightened, then rolled once more. I could feel my heart thundering in my chest. It was then I began to understand that this was a personal message sent directly to me, and that there could be wider consequences.

Lucy.

"My wife..." I stammered, barely able to articulate the words.

"I'm on my way, I'll go straight there," Wyatt said, all joking and bravado forgotten.

"You know where he lives don't you, Perkins?" Wyatt said as he pulled on his leather jacket.

"Yes, but..."

"Well come on, let's go."

"Who would do this, Martin?" Patterson said, which was funny as I didn't even notice him standing beside me. "Who would do this and why?"

I had no answer to that, and my brain, in no fit state to even attempt to figure it out, ignored the question. With shaking hands, I slid open my desk drawer and fished out the half pack of Berkley Superkings and silver lighter that I'd kept as a memento of my quitting smoking, and walked out of the door, leaving my colleagues gaping into the box that had been sent to me.

I knew I shouldn't, but I also knew I needed to have just one, to calm my nerves. It was in my mouth and lit almost before I got outside, that first drag not helping the nausea, but I willed it to pass all the same. Good god, that nicotine rush was worth it. I don't care what anyone says, that feeling is the best in the world. I sat on the curb outside, arms resting on knees, head down as I let the blessed cocktail of the cancer stick surge through me. My hands were shaking so much that I dropped the cigarette, which fell into the sewer grate at my feet. Unable to hold it back any longer, I threw up, retching into the very same grate and splashing my trousers and shoes with flecks of partially digested breakfast.

With nothing else left to eject, and ignoring the glances of passers-by on the street, I did what any man in my position would. Did I launch back into the building and into the investigation? Did I lead my team in demanding answers? Not exactly. I lit another cigarette and smoked it down to the tip, then another. By the fourth one, my throat was sore, but I didn't care. All that mattered is what the message meant, and who the hell would send it to me?

FRIDAY

12.

Detective Andrews had left my house, with his little friend, and yet I hadn't been able to get him out of my head. Here was the man charged with taking me down before I could do any more harm. Here was, for all intents and purposes, my enemy. All night I contemplated how to mess with his head. At first I wanted to remain anonymous to him. I wanted to stay off his radar so I could do what needed to be done. The sight of the badges, when they'd first flashed them, had caused me to panic a little - not that I showed it. At least, if I did, they didn't appear to have have picked up on it. But then the inner darkness, the one which had surfaced at work earlier in the toilets, returned, floating to the surface with little to no effort as though it had always been close by.

I was enjoying the attention I was being paid by the authorities. I liked the fact that I felt challenged. It made me feel good, special almost, and as the evening had progressed I couldn't help but want him to know it was me. Let him know that I had stood so close to him, talked to him, and yet he had walked away. I wanted him to realise that that had been his one chance to take me down and he'd missed it because he hadn't looked hard enough. Hell, all he'd had to do was to come further into my apartment and chances are he'd have seen the photos of the crime scene - before it was considered one - sitting there on my kitchen table where I'd left them last weekend. Even now, after yesterday's close call, they were still there. Well - not all of them - just one. I needed the others to make up my invitations with when my gallery opens.

I'd taken the majority of the Polaroid's, packed a bag of clothes along with some essential toiletries, all of the credit cards I'd secured over the months and that was it. Nothing else was needed. Nothing else was going to be missed from the house. And, just like that, I'd left the apartment with the knowledge that I was never going back. Neither there nor to work - both were off limits now.

It had been two hours after the police visit when I'd left the apartment. I'd thrown the two bags into the back of the car and driven to the old family home, taking the long route, making sure to double back on myself on regularly to be sure that I hadn't been followed. Not that I thought I would be. They wouldn't have arranged a tail at this stage of our relationship. They wouldn't go to that much trouble just because I'd dared drive past the hotel. Regardless I'd rather be safe than sorry. And now - now I had decided to play with the police - I needed to be even more careful than before. Ensure I didn't do something stupid to lead them straight to me.

When I got back to the house Mandy was pleased to see me. I think my energetic excitement had made her nervous, but I couldn't help myself. The thought of being so close to the person who wanted to send me to prison was overpowering but not nearly as much as the plans I'd made for the rest of the night. Of course I'd smiled, placed my bags down in the hallway, and of course I'd reassured her that there was nothing to worry about. I told her that, although I was there, she was still more than welcome to be my guest and that nothing had changed. It was then that she asked me whether I had been feeling okay. A fair question I guess as, looking back, I'd been acting differently to how she was used to but I had her now. I no longer needed to be the nice guy manipulating her into getting what I wanted. I didn't need to wear the mask anymore, in fact, the mask would ultimately have been the one thing which could have led to my downfall. Yesterday, in the toilets at work, I'd realised that. The mask was slipping and getting harder to hide behind.

I kept telling Mandy I was fine, promising her that everything was better now and how grateful I was that she was there. She smiled at me. At least, she smiled at first. Her smile had soon disappeared from her face, replaced with a look of sheer terror and panic as I wrapped my hands around her scrawny neck and crushed her windpipe as hard as I could. She was struggling there, with my hands around her throat, with her shadow dancing on the wall in the frantic flickering of the flame by her side. As she fought against my grip I couldn't help but be aware of my growing erection - that familiar stirring below which I'd always been so good at ignoring. I didn't have time to dwell upon that this evening though, as I had a lot to do and, by this point in my evening, I was only too aware that time ticked on.

Just as I had previously suspected, the girl was weak and didn't put up much of a struggle. She tried kicking and clawing at me. She attempted to hit me and even push me away but her exertions became increasingly weaker until her body just went limp. She'd only been prevented from dropping to the floor because of the vice-like grip I had on her. Despite her limp limbs, I still held my hands around her neck for a few minutes more. Just to be sure.

It was a new morning now and I had woken up with as much excitement buzzing through me as when I had come to bed the night before. Not just because of what I'd done but also because Detective Andrews would most likely have received his parcel by now. Mandy's pretty little eyes pulled from her equally pretty head whilst her body was still warm. I wondered whether there'd been any hint of life in her as I'd pulled them from their sockets. If so, had she seen what I was doing? I rolled over in what was once my parent's bed and looked at her corpse. "Did you get to watch me?" I asked her. No answer. How rude. I reached across with my right hand and turned her head towards me so that I could stare down into the empty eye-sockets. "Did you see what I was doing to you?" I asked her again. Another question unanswered. "Do you still see me?" I leant forward to her dead body and kissed her on the mouth. She didn't flinch away. I guess she doesn't see me anymore. Was just a thought anyway. Never spent so much time with a corpse before now. I have to confess, before all this kicked off, it's not something that I'd envisioned I'd ever do but... it's nice. It's peaceful. I experienced the same feeling back at the hotel room when I looked upon my art. Not only did I see a thing of beauty but I also felt peace. At the time, in the hotel, I didn't know what it was - what I was experiencing. I just knew I liked it. Last night, after dropping the parcel off to the police station, I felt it again. I sat down with the body for no other reason than to enjoy the moment and enjoy the feeling. It was then that I realised what the sensation had been. I had felt peace and, more worryingly, that before I'd started all this, I'd never really experienced it before. Not properly.

I'd taken the girl up the stairs to the bedroom, carrying her in my arms. The emotions that I'd felt with her around, I didn't want to forget or miss out on, so I thought it was the best thing to do.

This morning, lying with her, I didn't feel the same kind of peace. I felt something else - the sensation which had stirred yesterday at work, which had seen me run to the toilets to calm myself down. I'm feeling that again. I'm not fighting it though. I have to say, I'm enjoying it just as I eventually enjoyed it yesterday, when I wasn't standing somewhere so public.

I reached across to her body and cupped her breast - still covered by her bra and blouse. I half expected something within my brain to stop me from doing what I was doing, a little voice to tell me that it was wrong. But I heard nothing. Instead, there was a small voice which became louder the more I pressed against the bra's soft padding, telling me this feels nice. I sat up and ripped her blouse open, revealing the cotton bra which I had previously seen when the girl thought it was what I'd wanted. I felt those same strong feelings which had stirred the day before so it wasn't long before I pulled the bra down to reveal her pert, pale breasts. They're perfect if not a bit cool to the touch. I gave them both a squeeze.

Urges stirred inside, encouraging me to go further. I felt as though I was no longer myself. I felt like a new person. Someone I couldn't control, nor really wanted to. I jumped up from the bed and feverishly pulled at her gray skirt which ripped off with ease, showing her white cotton panties, stained through days of living on the streets. The thought of the girl's father popped into my mind - albeit briefly -

and I couldn't help but think what kind of sick bastard would do that to their own daughter. As I said, a brief thought as I found myself ripping the panties away to reveal a tainted pussy and the beginnings of an unkempt bush. A girl of her age, clearly having not experimented too much with styles, had left it to do its own thing. Fair enough. Had her life been fair, she would have had all the time in the world to decide what she was comfortable with and, who knows, maybe she would have preferred the natural look as opposed to trimming back or having a Brazilian. The thoughts receded from my mind. Instead all I could think about was how fucking hot it looked. Her father - clearly a man of taste.

Taste.

I leant forward and breathed in the rotten scent. I'm not sure how long she'd been on the streets, or how long she'd gone unwashed, or whether the smell was just because of her death. All I knew was that I was more turned on than I'd ever been before and I liked it. Before I knew what I was doing I flicked my tongue across the slit.

Salty.

My excitement grew. Using two fingers I parted her lips and let my tongue dart, briefly at first, inside. I wasn't sure whether it was death which tasted so delightful or whether it was the remnants of her natural juices. The leftover fragrance of a once innocent girl. A few more laps of my tongue before I kissed my way up her body, spending a little more time than entirely necessary at her bullet-like nipples. In death was she turned on by what I was doing? Or is this the start of rigor-mortis? The latter I guessed. Her limbs had been extremely stiff to move and I'm sure - when I forced them - I heard cracks from underneath the skin. Are bones breaking? Is that possible?

Forget about it. Not important. She won't care if they are breaking just as I won't care so long as she is tight. A few kisses on her neck before I pulled, gently, at her chin to open her mouth - just enough to give my tongue the space needed to slip in. I was surprised by the force needed to part her mouth but I got there in the end. I stopped kissing her long enough to spit into my hand. Spit which I rubbed into her young cunt before using the same hand to guide myself into her tight vagina. No need for protection. Not with this one. I sighed as the saliva helped me slip in. She feels good. Tighter than the whore I fucked. Certainly as tight as I had imagined. Is that because of her being dead or because of her being so young? I didn't care as I started to thrust backwards and forwards, all the time looking directly into the dark sockets of her empty eyes; my mind going back to what it had been like digging my fingers into their sides to pull them out, remembering how much I'd enjoyed it and the hard-on that it had earned me at the time. I couldn't help myself but to move up slightly and rim each of the sockets in turn. The excitement, the lust, the tightness of her cunt enveloping my prick, became too much and I ejaculated hard.

I didn't roll off her. I just stayed there, staring into the sockets with my penis deep inside her, still twitching from the powerful orgasm. She's still so pretty. Even like this. The perks of being young, I guess. Such beautiful skin. I had a perfect idea as to how she'd be displayed. I smiled, and withdrew my cock, letting my sperm drip onto the bedding beneath.

Today is shaping up to be a good day. I wonder how Detective Andrews is getting on.

FRIDAY

13.

They'd insisted I go home early, not that I would have stayed after what had happened.

Patterson drove me home, and both Perkins and Wyatt were there with Lucy when I arrived. It was obvious she'd been crying, but appeared a lot calmer now.

"We'll shoot off, Martin," Wyatt said, flicking his eyes towards Patterson.

"Yeah, thanks," I heard myself say from some distant place.

"Come on Perkins," the burly Scott said, heading for the door. "Let's leave these two in peace."

I was impressed. It was the longest I've heard him speak without an F- or C-bomb spewing out of his mouth.

"Are you sure you don't want us to leave an officer outside?" Patterson said then, looking at me with what appeared to be genuine concern.

"No, it's okay, don't worry." I replied, still in that distant place in my head.

Patterson leaned close enough so that I could smell the mint on his breath and the cheap aftershave on his skin.

"Lock the door after we leave. I'll personally make sure we find out who did this."

He gave my arm a squeeze, and then looked beyond me to Lucy, who was cradling her coffee like it was the only thing anchoring her to the world.

"Look after her, Martin. This has been a big shock."

"I will."

"And for god's sake, take a few days off will you? Let us handle this."

I nodded, knowing well enough that it would be easier said than done. I let Patterson out, locked the door behind him. What happened next was completely unexpected. Pigs flew. Hell froze over. And Martin Andrews began to cry. As I slid down the door onto my haunches, that stupid Pringles advert jumped into my mind again. I had popped, and didn't know if I would be able to stop.

A half hour later, eyes red and sore, I had relocated to the more comfortable sitting room, and was cradling a coffee. Lucy sat beside me, just watching me and waiting until I was ready to talk. I love that about her, how she always knew when to speak and when to just be quiet. Too many couples feel the need to fill every waking moment with chatter. For me, the true strength in a relationship is when two people can just sit together in the same room and not feel the need to talk. I took a sip of my coffee, desperate to organise my thoughts into some kind of rational order.

What had happened was every police officer's worst nightmare. As a rule, we tend to upset a lot of people. A lot of them threaten us, of course, but most are empty words, thrown by idiotic pricks who think they are some kind of big time gangster. We are taught early to let the words slide, to not be drawn into conflict with these arseholes. However, it seemed that every now and again, things would go a little bit too far, and situations became personal. I took another sip of coffee: it was a touch too sweet, but still felt good as it warmed me. My brain screamed for nicotine, but despite indulging it earlier, I was determined to get back on track. And besides, all of that was just a distraction from the conversation I'd been dreading since I'd found out about the pregnancy.

I put my cup on the floor, and half-turned towards her.

God, I felt bad. I'd been acting like a complete dick for months now, and yet she was still there, waiting for whatever I needed from her. It shouldn't be so hard to open up to this woman, someone who was my entire world. I didn't know how much about the case Wyatt or Perkins had told her, but I suspected not that much. She was obviously concerned about me, I could see it in the way she was frowning and rubbing her thumb and forefinger together the way she did when she was nervous. It was awful to see, but nowhere near as bad as I knew she would be if she knew what had actually happened. First things first though, I had some serious explaining to do.

"What's going on Martin?" she asked, perhaps sensing my willingness to talk.

Hesitation.

That stubborn tongue of mine had gone into business for itself again, and was refusing to play ball. Just when I was about to go into panic mode and try to think of something else to say, it sprang to life, forming the words that I'd wanted – no, needed - to say for the last five months.

"I'm scared that we're making a mistake by bringing a baby into this world."

I blurted it out before I talked myself out of it, and knew that her reaction would be key to how the rest of our chat would go.

She smiled and took my hands, and turned those gorgeous blue eyes onto mine.

"It'll be okay, everything will be fine. I worry too. The world is full of bad people, but you have to remember there are good people out there too."

"Not as many as you think," I croaked, struggling to hold back the emotion that suddenly seemed ready to explode out of me. "I just want you to be safe."

"We will be, but you can't do it all. Not by yourself."

I saw a vision of those skewered eyes that had been sent to me and almost screamed, or cackled. I wasn't sure which it would be, so I swallowed it down.

"I have to try. I keep thinking that if I work hard enough, and I get enough of them off the streets…" I trailed off, knowing that my voice was wavering.

"You always do this Martin," she said, squeezing my hands. "You get so involved, so deeply into things once you set your mind to them. Sometimes you have to come up for air before you drown."

I nodded, fighting a losing battle to keep the wet stuff inside my tear ducts.

"What happened today at the station? Why did those officers come over here in such a hurry?"

Here it was. The knife edge. Black or white, truth or lie. My next words would set the tone for the rest of the conversation, and although I was sick of lying, I also knew that the truth as it was would be just too much for her to bear. Instead, I chose to tell the truth without filling in all the details. It was a middle ground that I could live with.

"I'm investigating a case, and I received a threat through the post. It's nothing to worry about."

Her eyes changed, and I was more certain that keeping the details of my macabre delivery from her was the right one.

"What kind of threat? Are we in danger?"

"Just verbal stuff. Nothing to worry about. We aren't in any danger."

Art

I hated lying, then reminded myself that it was justified. She couldn't know about the package I'd been sent. Not until I had come to terms with it and what it meant.

"Who would threaten you, and why?"

"That's what we plan to find out, and we will. I just wanted to make sure you were safe, hence the hoopla earlier. I didn't mean to scare you."

She pulled her jumper over her thumb and wiped the tears from my eyes.

"It's okay, I... I've never seen you open up like this before."

"I know, and believe me, it's something I'm working on improving. Just give me a little time, that's all I ask."

"I understand, and appreciate you trying. I knew you were never the forthcoming type right back from when we first met. I knew what I was getting into."

She even managed a smile: in spite of everything she was still coping better than I was. I knew then, even if I couldn't say it, that I loved her more than anything, and would do anything to protect her.

"I was younger back then," I shot back with a smile of my own. "More hair and less stomach."

"I love your hair just the way it is, gray flecks and all."

"Careful, you might give me a complex."

It was nice, that natural banter between us which had been missing for a while. Odd that it took such a bizarre set of circumstances to bring us to this point, but I was grateful nonetheless. Now if only I could solve the riddle of what kind of psycho saw fit to send me my nasty little package, I could almost start believing in life again.

"Martin?"

I blinked and looked at her. She had obviously said something to me as I was zoned out.

"Sorry, I was miles away, say again?"

"Are we going to be alright?"

"Of course. We always are."

Perhaps my mask of a smile had managed to convince her, as she hugged me, holding me tight. I returned the favour, enjoying our closeness. Glancing down to the bump of her stomach, I started to ask myself if I was really that happy. Of course, Lucy was everything to me, it was just the rest of my life that seemed to be in the toilet. There were a frustrating number of counterarguments for everything I could come up with. My job was high pressure and low pay, but it was secure, and if today had proved anything, it was that I had colleagues who cared about me and my well being. Financially, I could afford to get another job, but that could all change when the baby arrived. I had been reliably informed that they were a shitting, eating, financial black hole, so perhaps staying put – even with the attention of whatever nut sent me that box - was the right call.

Lucy and I snuggled down, just enjoying the silence and each other's company. I tried not to think about work, but as always, my wife was right, and something in me seemed hard-wired to make me a hopeless workaholic.

As much as I really didn't want to deal with it, the day's events were weighing heavily, perhaps given room to fester by finally opening up to Lucy and getting some of that clutter out in the open. Something was niggling at me, and that instinct within told me there was something I was overlooking, some vital piece of information I was missing which would open this thing up and point me in the right direction. I just couldn't put my finger on what.

Instead of dwelling on it, I grabbed the remote and switched on the TV. Maybe staring at that thing for a few hours would let my mind rest for long enough to pick out what it was that was troubling me. I hoped so. Despite Patterson giving me the okay to take a few days off, I knew that I would be in the office first thing. Don't judge me, it's just how I am.

SATURDAY

14.

The taxi I called from my mobile - an old pay as you go phone I'd found in one of the cupboards at home - picked me up from the end of my drive as requested. I hated this phone. Ugly thing, and tricky to navigate. Definitely a brick. But I couldn't risk using my own mobile - not yet anyway. Can't risk the police tracing me until I'm ready for them to do so. For now I need to remain anonymous.

I slid it into my pocket while climbing into the taxi, wondering whether it would be worth using one of my 'naughty' credit cards to buy a better handset. Probably not needed. A bit over the top considering how much time I had left...

"Where to, mate?" the driver asked. He barely paid me any attention, which was good. I'd counted on that. Didn't want him recognising my face should he see it again. He'd just given me a quick glance, via the rear-view mirror, as he'd asked the question.

"Anywhere along the High Street in town is fine." I replied, sitting back and making myself comfortable for the journey. My face was half-hidden by the hooded top and scarf I was wearing. One of the benefits of foul weather being that it was easier to hide under layers and layers of clothes without raising any eyebrows. Couldn't get away with that in the summer months - not that I'd planned it this way. Just a happy coincidence.

I still hadn't finished with the girl, even two days after I'd put her out of her misery and made her immortal. Instead I'd left her in the bed where she continued to stain the bed sheets with her rotting fluids. As I sat back, memories of yesterday morning flashed through my mind, specifically of what I'd done to the girl. As much as I wanted them to, the memories didn't stop there. Instead I remembered being at work the other day, and what I'd done in the toilets and, on top of that, what I'd done to the girl in the hotel. It wasn't the fact that I'd committed murder which plagued my thoughts; I didn't think of it like that. I was creating art. The women's deaths had been necessary so if anything I'd rendered the pair a favour. The whore wouldn't have had to lower herself to fuck men for money anymore and the runaway teen wouldn't have to keep running from her fuck of a rapist father. What troubled me most was that I had completely lost control on both occasions - unable to stop myself from fucking them. Even now, sitting in this warm taxi, I couldn't understand where those sudden urges to carry out the acts had stemmed from. I've never been a sexual person. Even before I came to realise the kind of monster I was - at least the one dwelling within me - I was never a sexual being; my passions driven more by pieces of art and... darker thoughts.

Whereas my school colleagues had all lost their virginity around the age of fifteen and sixteen, I hadn't lost mine until I'd been in my twenties and, even then, it had been by accident. I'd booked a whore. Not for the purpose of bedding her but because I had felt the urge to bash her brains in with a rock I'd found amongst the woodlands close by my flat. I'd called the girl up, having found her advert in the back of a magazine, and then invited her to my apartment. The plan was simple and crude; she'd be invited in and then, when she asked for the money, I'd just hit her. The blow would have knocked her to the floor and I would have just kept hitting her until her head, and face were no longer recognisable as human. I don't know why I'd felt the urge. I remember feeling it build deep within me for a long time but, to this day, I still didn't know where it had initially come from or why it had been there. I just remember it getting stronger and stronger until I was unable to take it anymore and felt that, if I didn't act upon it, I'd go insane. I can't explain it and I certainly won't try and excuse myself for it. That was who I was at the time just as now, this is who I am with regards to making my sculptures.

Needless to say it didn't happen the way as I'd imagined it. The girl came to the house. She asked for the money. I wanted to hit her, I really did, but I couldn't. Something held me back, some last straw of sanity perhaps which became broken some time later without me even realising it? Instead of delivering a blow to her head, I found myself delivering cash to her hand. And then one thing led to another. I came - eventually - but I wouldn't say I enjoyed it. At the same time I can't say I didn't enjoy it. I didn't feel anything. Not at the time. Hours later, though, I remember feeling down that I hadn't done what I had originally planned to do. Bash her head in with a rock.

Yesterday though, on more than one occasion I would hasten to add, as well as in the hotel and bathroom - I enjoyed myself. The sexual side of things felt just as important to me as the need to create art and it's not that which was scaring me now. When I was taking what I needed from the two women, for my art, I was very much in control. I was decisive. I did what I had to do. I got the job done and

I'm fine with that but, with regards to the sexual side, I had no control whatsoever. None. And that lack of control concerns me more than anything else. A lack of control is something which could quite easily get me caught.

"Must cost a fortune!" the taxi driver suddenly said. He still wasn't looking at me. Instead he was paying attention to the roads. I watched him via his reflection in the rear-view mirror waiting for him to continue but he didn't say anything else to justify his outburst.

"What's that?" I asked, caving with the need to know what he was talking about.

"Living out here and not having a car. It must cost a fortune with taxis and such like. You'd be better off moving closer to town or learning to drive," he said. I wasn't sure if he was being particularly stupid and trying to annoy me or whether he really believed I didn't have a car. Perhaps just bored and fishing for information?

"Car didn't start." I told him. It wasn't necessarily a lie. After all, the car really didn't start, but only because I hadn't put the key in the ignition. Still, he didn't know that. In fact, before calling the taxi company, I'd nearly jumped into my car without thinking to drive back into town to get what I required: luckily I remembered the police knew the registration, make and model and might be looking for me after the stunt I'd pulled with the parcel.

I wasn't stupid enough to think they'd immediately connect me with it but at the same time I wasn't naïve enough to think the thought hadn't crossed their minds. After all – what were the chances of them questioning me (and potentially only me) and then having that show up the next day? And if they did suspect me of sending the package then it wouldn't be long before they went to my apartment and found the next little present I'd left them - the photograph of the original piece. Soon after that, every police officer in the area would be on the lookout for my vehicle. In hindsight I probably should have waited a couple of days before sending the little gift to the detective but then I figured it wouldn't really make much of a difference. I'd wanted a challenge and now I had one. Besides which, I'll always be one step ahead of them. I'll always be the one with the clear advantage. Just as long as I kept my recently awakened sexual urges under control.

"What's wrong with it?" the taxi driver asked.

I shrugged, "Not a mechanic." My short answer was enough to make him go quiet again but not for long.

"Probably the cold weather and rain. My car doesn't start sometimes. Gets damp. Usually the spark plugs." I wasn't sure whether he was trying to be helpful or just irritating. If he was being helpful then he was failing. I considered leaning forward and yanking the steering wheel from his hands, forcing the car from the road into one of the many trees which lined the tarmac. The only reason I didn't was because I'd have come off worse than him. "A cheap fix if it is that," he continued.

"I'll bear that in mind," I lied.

"Much planned in town then?"

He was starting to irritate me but I slipped the social mask on because the police knew what I looked like as well as what I drove. I was pretty sure I had removed any photographs of me from the apartment (not that there were many) but, even so, they might have been able to do a police sketch of what I looked like and release it to the public. Worst case scenario they'd track down where I worked and I was one hundred percent sure there was an image of me on their computer system. A picture taken when I'd first gotten the job. Identification purposes. The one loose end I was unable to tie up, much to my disappointment. If I was rude to the taxi driver there was more chance of him remembering me. Yes I was buried under a hood and a scarf but, even so, there could still be a chance he'd spot a similarity to a picture in the news if it came down to it. I couldn't take that chance.

"Shopping."

"Nice. Early start of Christmas presents?" he asked.

"Yes," I lied.

I was actually heading for the sex shops. Nothing to do with my awakened, horny urges and everything to do with it being the best place to secure some much needed restraints. If I wanted to start collecting specimens for the rest of my projects then I'd need something to keep them all secured with until I was ready to work on them. Unfortunately, I'm sure not all of my subjects were going to come as easily to me as the pretty runaway girl had.

"Good for you. I always say I'm going to start my shopping early but never do. Christmas eve soon comes around and I find myself snowed under with work and go panic-buying around whatever shops are still open!" he laughed, "Last year some of the presents I bought ended up coming from petrol stations. Have to say, the wife wasn't too happy."

Had I not had a scarf covering half of my face I'd have smiled at him out of politeness. Luckily I didn't need to.

"Any ideas what you're looking for?" he continued. Jesus, he's relentless.

"Nope." I just wanted to tell him to shut up. I wanted to ask whether there was any medication he should have been taking for his constant verbal diarrhoea but I knew I couldn't. The most frustrating taxi ride in the history of bad taxi journeys. Before now I'd been on long rides where the driver wouldn't even grunt at me. I wanted some peace and quiet, to get my head around what else I needed to do and here I was, stuck with the most chatty fucker I'd ever had the displeasure of meeting.

"Well so long as you avoid the petrol stations, I'm sure you'll be fine."

Much to my relief we both slipped into a comfortable silence for the remainder of the drive into town. Perfect time for me to sit back and consider the many things I still needed to obtain for my prestigious art gallery.

The electricity, water and gas had come back on yesterday but most of the bulbs had blown, so I definitely need to get some of those. I want the guests to have a clear view of my works after all. So I needed bulbs, and restraints from the sex shop for starters. Handcuffs would do. Maybe some under bed restraints if they're cheap enough. I paused a moment as my mind wandered back to the idea of bulbs. I need some for the house - definitely - but what about extra spotlights too? Portable ones? Something which could help me play around with light and shadows? Yes, definitely a good idea and something else to invest in. After all, it made no sense sparing any money if I want to make the most striking exhibition possible. I also needed to get a van from somewhere - some hire company I guess - so I could pick up my latest specimens. I didn't dare risk doing so in my car. I'm more than ninety percent positive they aren't looking for it - just me being paranoid and probably still slightly regretting sending the parcel. A little bit anyway. Part of me still feels proud about that move.

Anyway, put that from my mind. Keep focused. I needed some restraints and bulbs, plus a new suit so I can look good for the opening night of the gallery. I didn't want people taking my picture with me looking a wreck. That wouldn't do at all. And I should get a decent tool kit, something to help sculpt my pieces. Some metal poles from a D.I.Y store, perhaps, and fishing wire in case any of them need support. It wouldn't look professional if any of them fell over.

And more food. As a rule, I don't eat loads but I'll still need to pick some extra up. Could even get some frozen, or chilled, bits and pieces now that the fridge-freezer is back on. So much to do in so little time. The thought of putting more pressure on myself, by sending the package to the police, sneaks into my mind again. I shake it off.

Other than those things I think that's it, other than the required people, but I won't be getting them until I know for sure that everything else was ready and, more importantly, I had a plan on how to get them without causing alarm to anyone who could be passing by. Whoever these people end up being, I just need to be able to make them disappear quickly and quietly. My mind kept warning me that, when I start, everything will fall into place extremely quickly and I need to be ready for anything and everything.

SATURDAY

15.

Walking around town I couldn't help but feel as though people were looking at me as if they recognised me. A feeling of paranoia flowed through my veins. I couldn't help wondering whether they knew me because of what I'd done at the hotel and what I'd sent to the detective. Had word got around already? No. It couldn't have. Besides, in the unlikely event the police had put two and two together already, I'm sure people would be screaming rather than just staring. Ignore them. They're probably not even looking at me. It's more likely to be a casual glance so as to avoid walking into me, the same way I looked at other people when I walked through crowded streets. Okay, mostly the same way I look at other people. After all, there were times when I looked at them and wondered what their head would look like on a pole. Mind you, they could be having the same thoughts. Nothing would surprise me anymore. Regardless, they're not looking at me because they know me. They don't. I'm nothing more than a face in the crowd. For now, at least. Put these poisonous thoughts to the back of my mind and focus on where I need to be.

The first store I walked into was the high street sex shop which hid its true intentions by selling some pretty lingerie at the front of the store. People knew it wasn't a shop just for lacy underwear though and the ones who actually chose to visit the premises, well, they were mainly going in for the sex toys sold at the back. The further into the store you went, the more extreme the toys.

I walked through to the back, right by the cheerful assistant who greeted me as I'd come in. She wished me a good morning. I grunted at her. A fair exchange and one which didn't stop her from following me to the more extreme of the sex toy range.

"Was there anything in particular you were looking for?" she asked. I looked at her. I couldn't help but wonder what sort of woman would choose to work in a shop like this. Would mummy and daddy be proud of their little girl? I could hear the conversations now...

And how's your daughter? What's she doing now?

She has a job selling plastic cocks.

Oh marvellous! Can she get me a discount?

"I'm good thank you," I told her. I'd hoped that would have been enough for her to leave me be, but she persisted in standing by me as I browsed the shelves of artificial cocks and other instruments meant to enhance one's sex life. The whole thing was foreign to me and, thankfully, one that I didn't need to worry about. I knew what I was after.

"If you're looking on behalf of your lady, I recommend this one!" The shop-girl reached across to the third shelf down and selected a large purple vibrator. Supposedly one of the top-sellers according to the label next to the price ticket. "I have one of these at home and it really hits the spot." She turned it on. "You can see how powerful it is just by pressing it against the tip of your nose." She held it up for me to put my own nose against it. I declined.

"Sorry - that's what I'm after..." I pointed to the restraints which hung to the side of the sex toys. There were normal handcuffs, furry handcuffs, the under bed restraints that I'd previously considered, ball gags and a few bits and pieces which I didn't recognise and certainly wasn't about to ask about having seen the girl's enthusiasm at demonstrating the vibrator. She raised her eyebrows and made a funny ooh noise from her mouth, as if she hadn't expected me to have chosen such items. Did I really not come across as the sort of person who'd buy this kind of thing? I'm not sure whether that was a good thing or a bad thing.

"A fun choice!" she said with a knowing smile. Of course she knew. I wondered whether there was anything in here she hadn't sampled and experimented with. "Anything specific in mind?" I pointed to the classic handcuffs. Metal. Lockable. Nothing fancy needed. She smiled and pulled a pair off the display hook for me. As she handed it to me she asked, "Is there anything else?"

I looked down at the handcuffs. They're definitely rigid enough. "I'll take all of the pairs hanging there," I told her. For the first time since meeting me she looked startled. I quickly adjusted society's mask for her, "I run a brothel. They're a popular choice!" I flashed her a smile. She nodded, smiled back, and handed me the rest of the handcuffs. "I think that'll do for now," I told her.

SUNDAY

16.

The digital clock told me it was 4:17am. The alarm wasn't due to go off for another hour or so, but I'd snapped awake nonetheless. That thing... the thing which had been bothering me, that niggling bit of information that just wouldn't present itself, chose 4:17am as the moment to make an appearance. The room was dark and draped in shadows, I could hear the steady probing tap of drizzle on the windows punctuated by Lucy's steady breathing next to me, but more than that, I'd connected the dots. Scored a goal. Dotted the I's and crossed the T's.

That familiar surge of adrenaline and fear raced through me, and I knew then that my previous half-hearted attempts to convince myself I wanted to change jobs was never going to happen. We were slaves to each other, like the snake eating its own tail. We were one, we were the same.

The epiphany was so obvious, so blatant that I didn't know quite how I'd managed to miss it. Maybe the stress of the situation had been a factor. Either way, I knew now and had to act.

I slid out of bed and dressed in the dark, an act that I had become so accustomed to over the years that it barely slowed me down. Hurrying to the bathroom, I kept repeating the connection over and over and over in my head.

They were the same. They were connected.

The girl in the hotel had been on display. And the box which had been left for me with the note saying 'See me' had come from the same person.

Had whoever done it expected fanfare? Or perhaps worldwide news coverage of his despicable act? Had he, upon seeing that his handiwork had been ignored and gone unreported felt compelled to send another message, one that would be much harder to shove away.

Was 'see me' a question posed by someone looking to toy with the police, or was it the frustrated command of a man furious that his work had gone unnoticed?

Yes.

It all made sense now. One by one, the pieces were starting to fit.

It was him.

The man who had driven past the hotel. Not to assess its suitability for him and a girl, but to check on why his carefully placed (displayed) creation wasn't being acknowledged.

The man who, when questioned, had seemed so calm and assured, but also could not have known he'd made an error. He didn't know that he was, so far, the one and only person who had been questioned as a possible suspect, and as a result the only person who knew that I was in charge of the case.

I even gave him a card so he knew where to find me.

I always liked that Sherlock Holmes quote from 'The Sign of Four.'

'When you have eliminated the impossible, whatever remains, however improbable, must be the truth.'

If it was good enough for Arthur Conan Doyle, it was good enough for me.

I think I have him.

I think I've found our killer.

* * *

A lot of police officers would tell you that the idea of getting scum off the streets is the best thing about being on the force. It wasn't. It's the moments like this. These adrenaline-fuelled breakthroughs. The euphoria which comes with it always made me wonder if we were as addicted to that high as some of the scumbags we locked away. They called it chasing the dragon, but now I was chasing something altogether more violent. I know it's stupid, and I should have phoned it in, but I had to know for myself. I had to prove I was right before I let Patterson in on what was happening. So, instead of racing off to the station like I knew I should, I went to Benton's flat. I had to do it. If only this was America. I could have gone in with my trusty firearm blazing. This being England, however, we didn't arm every police officer to the teeth and give him a license to maim at will. Consequently, I went up there with nothing but my anger that this prick had seen fit to try and terrorise me. Not the greatest idea I'd had, but sometimes good sense takes a back seat.

I reached his door, and that was the first time my anger subsided long enough for the fear to take hold. As harmless as he looked, if this guy was the one responsible for the hotel murder, then I had to acknowledge that he was dangerous. I wanted to kick the door down, and it took a huge effort not to do it. Instead, I put my head to the door and listened, all the time shooing away images of him on the other side, jamming a knife through the flimsy wood and into my brain. I couldn't hear anything. No TV. No sounds of anyone shuffling around in there. My instinct was screaming to be heard, telling me to go to Patterson and get a warrant to search the place. It was the next logical step, but logic and I had never been the greatest of friends, so I did something that would have my academy instructors shaking their heads. I pounded on the door and waited to see if he would answer.

I stood there for a full minute in that piss-stinking corridor before I calmed down enough to realise that wherever he was, he wasn't home. That was actually a good thing, as it meant that my initial burst of anger (and yes, stupidity) could be rectified. I wasn't sure if I had enough evidence, but I had to approach Patterson about a warrant. If we could get inside, I was sure we could find something to tie the prick to the hotel murder at the very least. Taking a last look at the door, I headed for the stairs, quietly confident that Patterson would see that I had good cause for the warrant and make it happen.

* * *

"What do you mean, no?"

I couldn't believe the words coming from Patterson's mouth. I could only glare at him across the desk, clutching the arm rests hard enough to turn my knuckles white.

"We don't have enough Martin. Not for a warrant. We can't do it on a hunch. Granted, it's a strange coincidence, but no more than that."

"Come on boss, nobody but Benton knows I'm running point on this. It has to be him."

"I can't just let you do this, there are rules and…"

"Fuck the red tape," I spat. "This prick is threatening me personally. What if it was you?"

Patterson fidgeted. He looked flustered and, for a split second, I felt sorry for him, then I remembered the package, and knew I'd have to push for this if I wanted to put an end to it.

"Look, Martin, I can't just give you free reign to go search the place. We need something, some connection other than instinct."

"Can't you bend the rules? Especially considering how personal this has become. I thought I could rely on you."

I regretted saying it immediately, especially when I saw the pained look flash on Patterson's face.

"Martin, try to understand…"

"No, you try to understand! This prick is coming after me, and you sit there and talk about red tape!"

Patterson's face flushed an angry red at that. "I'm still your superior, and you will address me with the proper respect!"

We were both shouting, and it was a relief when Wyatt knocked on the door and stuck his head in the room. I could tell by the look on his face that he had heard it all and hadn't wanted to disturb us.

"What is it, Wyatt?" Patterson spat.

"Sorry to, err, interrupt boss. Phone call for Martin."

"Take a message and say he'll call back. We're in the middle of something here."

"I did say that boss, but… they insisted. Said it was urgent."

I wondered if it was Lucy, and I half stood. "I'll come and get it,"

"You can take it here," Patterson snapped, sliding his phone towards me. "You and I aren't finished talking yet. Patch it through here Wyatt."

"Yes boss," Wyatt said giving me a quick glance before ducking out of the office. A few seconds later, the phone rang. Under the watchful eye of Patterson, I picked it up, and in that instant, everything changed.

"Hello?"

"Detective Andrews?"

"Speaking. Who is this?"

"I need help..."

"Do I know you?"

"I just can't control myself. This isn't who I am..."

My stomach tightened and started to roll as realisation dawned on me. I hoped I was wrong, but that was put to rest with the next words which drifted from the handset.

"Last night I cut her skin off, that pretty little girl. I used a kitchen knife. It wasn't as perfect as I had wanted but it served a purpose..."

It was him. I recognised that twang in his voice. I told myself to stay calm, to keep him talking. My guts gave another greasy roll as I forced myself to be neutral in my response.

"It's you isn't it, Mr. Benton?"

"Her skin. I wrapped it around myself. Used it as a make-shift sheath..."

"What do you mean?" I heard myself ask, struggling to cope

with the unreality of it all.

".... I pleasured myself."

"You need to turn yourself in. If you don't, you know what will happen." I could barely concentrate. He was so calm, so matter of fact in the way he spoke. If not for the fact that I had already seen what he was capable of, I would have been inclined not to believe him.

"I can't. I'm not finished yet. You want their deaths to be meaningless?"

"They already are. Whatever it is you are trying to achieve, it won't work. I'll find you, I'll catch you. Nobody will ever remember you. Turn yourself in before it gets worse."

I was shaking. Maybe Patterson could see it in my face, because he was no longer angry. Instead, he was watching me, his mouth hanging open. His expression made me wonder just how bad I must have looked sitting across the desk from him.

"No. They're art. They'll be immortal thanks to me!"

"They're dead thanks to you. You have a chance to end this on your own terms. Trust me, you don't want the alternative. If I come after you, you'll only make things worse for yourself."

"Worse for myself? I'm making it better for myself. I'll be known across the world. My work will be known everywhere."

"If it's fame you want, then it won't happen. I'll personally make sure this is kept under wraps. We will deny everything. Nobody will ever know you did these things. Nobody will ever know you existed. Six months from now, you will be rotting in a prison cell just as anonymous as you are now."

"You can't."

I could hear a ring of uncertainty in his voice, and although I was in no way following protocol, I couldn't override the anger that raged through me. I didn't intend to respond, but the words were out of my mouth before I could stop them.

"You really must be stupid. Look around you. The world is a fucking cesspit of murder and crime. You think you might be the next Bundy or Dahmer, but they did what they did in a world that was unprepared. Let me tell you something, Damon. In this city alone, people die every day. Murders. Rapes. Assaults. Society is desensitised. Nobody will know you. Nobody will care. Nobody will ever know what it is you tried to do. You need to turn yourself in now, before it's too late."

"You should thank me. You'll be famous too. You'll be my best piece."

A look of revulsion passed over Patterson's face, and I knew why. I could feel my skin contorting, and although I was aware of it, I had no idea why. I was smiling.

"You don't scare me. You think you are the first loon to get personal. I won't rest. I won't sleep until I find you and bring you in.

That I can promise you. There is nowhere that you can hide where I won't look."

"Find me? When the time comes - you won't have to find me. I'll be the one presenting you with a glass of champagne..."

I opened my mouth to respond, but the line went dead in my ear. I set the phone back in its cradle and looked at Patterson.

"That was him wasn't it, the killer?" he said.

"It was Benton," I replied, locking eyes with him.

"You can't be sure…"

"I recognised his voice, Sir. When I called him by name, he didn't deny it. He said he intends to do more. Said he isn't finished yet. We need to act on this."

Patterson sat back in his seat, hands folded over his chest.

"Okay, I think we can get a warrant on this. Let me make some calls and see what I can do."

I nodded, but inside I was elated.

"This guy has obviously got some personal vendetta against me. I want to get Lucy somewhere safe until we have him."

"Good idea. Get yourself off home and fill her in. Is there somewhere she can go?"

I nodded. "She has a sister up north. I can get her to go up there for a few days."

"Then go now, and take Wyatt with you. Safety in numbers and all."

I nodded and stood, feeling guilty for my earlier outburst.

"Thanks boss. Sorry for losing it, it's just…"

I trailed off as he waved a dismissive hand.

"Forget it. If I took it personally every time someone got pissed off, I wouldn't have any friends. Go on, get home, and get that wife of yours safe. I should have your warrant ready to go by the time you get back."

I walked to the door, wondering just how things had become such a mess. I grabbed Wyatt, and then we were off, heading out of the station and heading home. I didn't want to lie to Lucy again, but it had to be done. I couldn't let her know how serious things had become.

I only hoped she understood.

SUNDAY

17.

I slammed the payphone down and stepped away from it, wrapping my scarf around the lower section of my face again to protect both my identity and my skin against the cold bitter wind. I could feel the rage surging through my body. The audacity of Detective Andrews to think he could hide my work away from the world. I felt so hot that I didn't need my hood up, or the scarf but I knew I couldn't take them off. Especially now my plans had changed. That son of a bitch. The belief that he has the power to stop me from sharing my creations for all to see? I'd picked up the phone, looking for help after what had happened last night, but now I'm ready to embrace that side of me. Clearly it's a necessary evil that I must learn to live with if I am to go any further with who I want to be. Clearly the uncontrollable sexual urges go hand in hand with the darkness beneath the mask I wear. Should have known really. Can't believe it took the hot headed words of a nobody to make me realise that.

I looked across the road from where I was still standing next to the payphone. The police station was a hive of activity. Had he chosen his words correctly, I could have been swayed into walking in with my hands raised to the ceiling. I had done enough to make sure my work would be noted - what with the whore, the school girl and that lady I'd picked up last night. That lady, the large girl I struggled to get into the back of my van. Can't think about her now - no time. Need to concentrate on what I'm doing, especially seeing as I'm so close to Detective Inspector Andrews.

I didn't need to continue taking people. What I'd done with the whale and the school girl would have been enough to get me known across the world. I would have been happy to leave it at that although my original plan was to go further. I just didn't like the uncontrollable sexual urges. They worried me. They made me think I was sick. Wrong for performing such atrocities. But not now. Not now he'd challenged me. Not now he believes he was smarter than me. He isn't, not in a million years. If it hadn't been for the puzzle pieces I sent him, he'd still be standing at a crime scene, scratching his arse and wondering what to do. He's nothing. Less than nothing. For now at least. In time he'll become something but only because I'll make it happen for him out of the goodness of my heart. I want to show him that, at the moment, he is less than a tiny speck in this overpopulated shit-hole of a world but, in time, he'll realise what it's like to be known across the globe. Even if it was too late for him to enjoy it.

I won't give up. I'll carry on with what I'm doing and my original plan for a gallery; a grand opening with me standing in the middle of it all, dishing out champagne for all to enjoy as they wandered around admiring my creations.

I carried on watching the front door of the station for a few more minutes before I turned back to the van I'd rented yesterday afternoon, from a budget company close to the centre of town. Good hardy transport to get around in and, more importantly, transport people back to the house in, as the whale could testify. Or at least *could* have testified had she still had a tongue.

I jumped into the front seat. Couldn't see the police station's door from this angle so I had to use the side mirror on the passenger side. And speaking of passengers; the bloodied brick caught my eye. With a swift gesture I swiped it off the seat and onto the floor. Couldn't leave it on the seat, especially not whilst I was parked illegally. Any minute now someone could lean in and tell me to move. The last thing I need is for them to see the incriminating evidence.

My mind drifted back to the previous evening. I hadn't meant to bring anyone home with me. I'd just been going for a late night drive, down some nearby country lanes, just to get used to the van I'd rented. It had been the first time I'd driven a van. Quite a bit bigger than my car. I wanted to make sure I looked a natural behind the wheel. Didn't want to attract any unwanted attention. About twenty minutes into my drive, just as I was considering going home again to start work on the school girl, I spotted the whale walking towards me out of the darkness. She flagged me down and I stopped. Not much choice with her standing in the middle of the road, flapping around as if struggling to make it back down the beach towards the water.

Broken down a few miles back, she told me, and no signal on her phone to call for help.

My lucky day.

I invited her to climb in with the false promise of help. I couldn't help but remember feeling the suspension lower when she slipped into the passenger seat. This is a big girl. My mind had already realised she'd be perfect to go with what was left of the school girl. Just the right amount of flesh. She was thanking me the whole way back to a garage where I used yet another fake card to purchase a tow-rope, promising her a tow back to the garage, where they'd be able to take a look at her vehicle the following morning.

I could just get them to tow me, she had told me. Apparently I had done enough.

I told her it wasn't a problem and that it would save her a towing fee. I drove her back to where her car was stranded and attached the tow-rope to the car. It was then that I'd hit her around the back of the head with the brick (which was just lying around at the garage next to a big old skip full of building waste). The noise she made as she landed. I'm sure it echoed.

I'd opened the back of the van already. The task of getting her into the back wasn't quite as easy, due to the differences in our weights. In the end I rolled her to the rear of the van, so I didn't have to lift her quite as far. I knew at the time that it would have made more sense to get a smaller woman - or even a man as it would really made no odds for what I had in mind. The reason I didn't was because she was big enough to not need more people for the same piece. Her skin, with the skin I'd cut from the school girl, would be more than enough for the quilt.

And it was. By the time I'd finished flensing the skin off her fat corpse, I'd filled two large bin-liners. More than enough. And that was when it happened. I was about to throw the last piece of skin from the back of the van, where I'd cut the body up on some plastic sheeting - when an undeniable surge of lust hit me hard. Before I knew what I was doing my trousers were round my ankles and I was frantically masturbating using her ripped flesh as a sheath for my penis, the time to ejaculation being less than when I'd had the dead schoolgirl.

It wasn't until hours later, after finishing what needed to be done, that I began to dwell upon my sexual antics. What should have been a happy occasion on the completion of another piece of work had turned to a bitter one where I feared what I had turned into. This sexual predator so unknown to me. So uncomfortable, yet simultaneously so appealing.

Even now, thinking back to what I'd done, I felt dangerous stirrings below. Something new, though. They were easier to shake off. My mind switched back to wondering where the Detective was and whether he'd be coming out of the office any time soon having decided, again thanks to our chat, that it was high time I got to know my new-found friend. A smile crept across my lips. I should phone him back and thank him. It appears he's actually helped me. Just not in the way I thought he was going to.

A scream from outside the van. I looked out of the windscreen and saw a hooded figure running down the street, white trainers and blue sports pants with a white stripe down the leg, clutching a handbag under his arm. A lady was screaming for someone to help her but no one paid her any attention. At least, not in the way she was hoping. Instead they simply comforted her. I shook my head. This fucking world. I turned away and just in the nick of time too, as Detective Andrews stepped from the building with, I guess, one of his colleagues.

From across the road I couldn't hear what they were saying but it looked to be serious. No doubt acting upon my phone call. Even though I hadn't confirmed that I was Damon Benton they're probably heading to my apartment anyway. I wondered, without the call, would they have bothered?

I watched the two officers go to separate cars. Andrews in a crappy looking Escort. Funny. I expected him to drive something a little fancier. A Ford Gran Torino perhaps? His colleague shouted something across to him from the driver's side of what must have been his own car. Can't make out what is said but get a hint of a Scottish tone. Figures. Stocky and ginger-haired. Couldn't get more stereotypical.

I patiently waited as the two cars reversed out and headed into the busy traffic. When there was a suitable amount of distance between them and myself, but not enough with which to lose sight of them entirely, I jumped out of the van, with a parcel I'd snatched up from the foot well of the passenger side next to the bloodied brick, and ran towards the police station. I had planned on taking the parcel in with me when I was going to give myself up. I thought it would be more dramatic. Now I'm not surrendering... Well, seemed a shame to waste it - the off cuts of the whale - and I don't really want to take it home with me again so he may as well have it anyway. Not really sure how I'd fit that piece in with the theme I had in mind.

As I approached the front door an officer stepped from the building and I thrust the package, a medium sized box of substantial weight, into his hand. "Detective Andrews!" I said. I about-turned and hurried across the road again ignoring whatever it was the police officer had said. Something about fucking delivery drivers being lazy. I couldn't be sure and, truth be told, I didn't care. By the time I got back to the van I noticed the officer had disappeared back into the building, no doubt grumbling about having to be a postman. If only he knew...

I slammed the van door and looked up the street. There's substantial distance between myself and the detective now. More than I'd wished for. Not a problem. I'll just have to push through the traffic until I'm a little closer. The perks of being in a van - not many drivers bother to argue with you.

* * *

I was surprised when we carried on past the turn off which would have taken the officers to my apartment. And I'd continued to be surprised as we'd driven on for another fifteen or so minutes until we'd come to what appeared to be a nice middle class area. Bigger houses than the ones near my apartment. Plain and unspectacular but, at the same time, better than I'd been used to, with the exception of my family home but, well, those walls were tainted with bad memories. And now blood, I'd sniggered.

About a quarter of the way down this street the detective's car had turned into a driveway while leaving the other car to park in the closest available space. I'd driven past, simultaneously keeping my head down and my speed at a steady thirty. A check in my rear-view mirror and neither party had been watching me. Instead they were greeting a woman who'd come running out of the house and into the arms of the detective.

"Hello, Mrs Andrews."

The look on her face; she clearly loved dear Detective Andrews. The heroic husband helping to save the world from crime. Why would she love him? From where I was sitting, from what I saw on the news, he wasn't doing a very good job.

I shrugged. I really hoped she'd like what I had planned for her husband. Shame I couldn't ask.

SUNDAY

18.

As Wyatt and I entered the house I saw that knowing look on Lucy's face, and realised that on the good husband scale, I'd failed pretty much across the board. To his credit, my usually foul-mouthed colleague had offered to make a cup of tea, to give me ample opportunity to explain to my long-suffering life-partner why she would have to move out of our home. I'd sat her down on the sofa where only a couple of days earlier we'd gone through almost the exact same motions, only then it hadn't seemed quite so serious. It's funny how things could change in such a short space of time.

"I need you to go stay with Danni and Chris for a little while," I said, trying to remain calm but knowing that the look in my eye was betraying me.

"Why, what's happened?"

"I don't want you to worry, that's the important thing, but something has changed about that situation I told you about."

"About the case becoming personal?"

"Yes," I nodded, hoping my act of supreme confidence was working, that she wouldn't see the terror bubbling away under the surface. It was the first time in a while I was glad I was a good liar. "It seems somebody may have taken a personal interest in me, and just as a precaution, we have to move you out for a while."

She started to cry, and I felt like the worthless bastard that I was, immediately followed with the thought that this was all down to that bastard Benton.

"I knew this would happen," she said, wiping her eyes on the sleeve of her cardigan. "I knew it. How long do I have to go away for?"

"I don't know. As long as it takes until we can get him off the streets. We're working on it right now, and the man's our top priority."

Wyatt brought the drinks and set them down, then sat quietly in the chair. All credit to him. As crude and foul-mouthed as he is, he's a good guy.

"I can't just up and leave. What will I say to Danni? How will I explain?"

"I spoke to her on the way over from the station. She understands. Remember, this is just a precaution. I don't want you getting any more stressed than you already are."

"How will I get there, she lives so far away…?"

Her lip began to tremble, and I was stammering for an answer when Wyatt jumped in and saved me.

"I'll drive you there. Martin said its somewhere up north. I was heading that way this afternoon anyway, if that's okay with you?"

She looked at me, and I could see the questions in her eyes. Can this man be trusted? Is it safe? I gave her the merest of nods, and felt another glut of guilt for my impression of Wyatt as being a one dimensional lout.

"Thank you", she said to Wyatt, but watching me.

"It's only short term, but I'll feel better knowing you're away from this until it blows over."

"Martin, I want you to answer me this, and please, don't lie. Can you do that?"

I nodded, not sure what was coming, but dreading whatever it was.

"Are you in danger?"

There it was. The question I'd been asking myself all morning. On the one hand, I had seen this guy. He looked harmless, the kind of person you wouldn't notice in a crowded room, but on the flip-side, I'd witnessed the brutality he was capable of, and even though he may not be a physical threat as a person, I had to acknowledge that my life could well be at risk. I was half considering another one of those white lies that I'd grown accustomed to, when my usually stubborn tongue went into business for itself without warning.

"Yes, I think I could be."

I saw something in her break then, and as she started to sob, I was surprised to find that for once I didn't hate myself. Instead, all my fury was directed towards Benton.

"I'll uh, go wash these cups up and give you two a few minutes," Wyatt said, making a hasty retreat.

I held Lucy close to me, feeling absolutely powerless to do anything else but be there for her.

"I knew this would happen, you can't be putting yourself at risk like this,"

She was right of course, but what else could I do? This was the only job I'd ever known. The only job I was good at. I'm too bitter and cynical now to consider changing careers. Besides, Lucy had known what I did for a living when we first met, and although there were a few dangerous moments, this was the first time anything as serious as this had happened. I was about to relay all this to her when she sat up and looked at me, eyes red, lip trembling.

"I love you, and I just want you to be safe," she said, watching and waiting for me to say it back, to give her the reassurance she desperately needed. My mouth opened, closed. Opened again. I swallowed, my throat feeling as if it was lined with sandpaper.

"I know," I said, screaming at myself inside. "And I'll do whatever it takes to make you safe. Right now though, you need to go pack a bag. Take whatever you think you might need."

Feeling like a cold, heartless bastard, I stood up and left her sitting there on the sofa, still needing that reassurance from me which I was starting to think I was simply incapable of giving.

"Come on, let's get that stuff together."

I could see the defeat in her face, and maybe, just maybe a touch of doubt in the strength of our relationship.

"Okay, let me get a few things. I'll give you a ring when I arrive."

"No," I said, shaking my head. "No contact until this is resolved. And don't answer any number you don't recognise."

"Will that other officer be staying close by?" She asked, nodding towards Wyatt.

"No, it's just a drop off, then he has to be on his way. He's officially on leave as of today."

She nodded, and I knew her well enough to guess what she was thinking.

"Besides, it's better this way. The more anonymous you are the better. Remember, this is just a precaution, but the deeper under the radar you are, the better."

She nodded again, but I don't think she was convinced. Either way, it was the best I could do. We gathered some things together in an overnight bag then drove back towards the station. Wyatt was driving and I was up front. I didn't speak, but I could feel Lucy's uncertainty. Wyatt must have felt it, because he was the quietest I've ever heard him. He pulled up at the station, and I turned in my seat to face my wife.

"This will all be okay. You know that, don't you?" I said, hardly believing the words as they left my lying mouth.

She nodded, but couldn't look me in the eye. I made a promise to myself then. Promised that as soon as this was all over and resolved, I would make sure I put things right. No matter what it would take to do it, I would get this marriage back on track. Those three words crawled into my throat again, but as per usual, got no further. Instead I turned to Wyatt.

"Let me know when you get there, will you?"

"Aye, I'll check in once I drop her off. Do what you need to do at this end, and do it quick."

I had no answer to that either, and so with nothing left to say or do, I climbed out of the car, and watched it drive away. I would like to say I was thinking of Lucy and hoping she would be okay, but the detective in me had already taken over, and so, as I headed back inside the station, my only thoughts were of Damon fucking Benton.

I walked towards the lift. This time, in no mood to wait, I went straight for the door leading to the stairs. To my surprise, Perkins was heading out as I pushed the door open.

"I was just coming to get you," he said as he passed me. He waved a piece of paper in front of me. "Search warrant. Let's go see if this hunch of yours is right."

Elated and angry at the same time, I let the pneumatic door creak closed and followed Perkins to his car. With luck, we could snag this prick before he hurt anyone else.

* * *

Back at Benton's apartment, Perkins and I stood looking at the door. The adrenaline was flowing, and I pounded on the cheap wood with my fist.

"Police! Open up." I shouted through the door, before knocking again.

"He's not in."

Perkins and I looked to the right, and the slob of a woman who stood at the threshold of the apartment next door, a dirty, snotty kid held to her flabby body. She looked at us with a mix of apprehension and contempt that I'd come to expect from people like that. Below a certain income level, people tended not to trust the police.

"Do you know him, the tenant?" I asked. Keeping calm. Keeping neutral.

"Only in passing. I ain't seen him for a few days." She grinned, flashing her gappy, blackened stumps of teeth at me. The kid was starting to fidget, and she readjusted him in her arms.

"How do you know he's not in?" Perkins asked.

"Saw him leave, might have been yesterday or the day before. I can't remember. I was pissed off my face." She grunted, flashing that mouth full of rot at me.

Good god, I glanced at the kid and felt sorry for it. Before its life had even really begun, it was at a severe disadvantage with a beast like that for a mother.

"Thank you," I said, hiding my disgust. "Now please, go inside and lock the door."

Maybe it was the way I said it, or maybe she could see how serious the situation was in my expression, but she did as she was told. I heard the chain slide into place, shortly followed by the muffled sounds of her screaming at said poor child for not keeping still. Anyhow, back to business. I glanced at Perkins, and he nodded. We should have brought a ram of some kind, but in our rush we forgot. Still, the door barely looked to be standing, and I didn't think it would take much.

It gave on the second kick, the wood splintering as it crashed against the wall. At that second, fear was forgotten, as was self-preservation. The training took over, and like a well-oiled machine, Perkins and I entered the flat.

SUNDAY

19.

Underwhelming would be the best way to describe it. It looked to be a perfectly normal, if grubby, flat. The air was stuffy, but there were no tell-tale smells of death. No macabre displays or bloodstains on the wall. It could be any flat belonging to any single person in the world. But I knew this was our guy. I'm not sure how, but there was an aura, some kind of charge to the atmosphere which told me that our killer lived here. Goosebumps rushed up my arms, and when I glanced at Perkins, I saw that he too could sense it. Whoever Damon Benton was, whatever persona he chose to portray, I was confident that this was our first genuine glimpse of the real man behind it all. The evidence of it was everywhere: the single armchair, more worn down than any of the other furniture; dated, badly maintained décor; a tray containing a gravy-stained plate on the floor beside the chair. Alarm bells were ringing in my brain, and just like that, it happened. This was definitely our guy. I just knew it. Perkins and I did a preliminary sweep, making sure the place was empty.

"What do you think?" he whispered to me, peeking out of the grimy windows to the street below.

"Look around," I said, poking my head into the dingy bathroom smelling faintly of stale piss. "It looks like he left in a hurry."

Perkins nodded, and went into the bedroom. I checked the living room first. Despite everything, the layout painted a picture of a very private, very lonely existence. I could only imagine what it would be like to stay here alone, sitting in the chair, staring at the TV and attempting to ignore the sounds coming through the paper thin walls from the other apartments. It would be easy to feel anonymous, it would be easy to want the world to acknowledge your existence.

I wondered how many nights he had sat here, in the dark, just listening. Maybe to the fat woman from next door screaming at her kid, or maybe someone upstairs, the floor rocking as they fucked, or argued, or played music. How long would it take for absolute isolation to trigger a man to kill in order to make the world take notice?

Not liking where that particular train of thought was taking me, I pushed it aside and made my way into the kitchen. It was as bleak as the sitting room, With faded yellow lino and an ancient cooker way past its best. There was a faint smell of old grease and rotten food. I took it all in, remembering my training. Observe. Catalogue. I could see the side of a grubby fridge-freezer tucked away in the corner. I was tempted to rush, but that was how things got missed and wankers like this walked free. Taking a deep breath, I started to look around. I was determined to be methodical and take my time. The cupboards were bare apart from a half-pack of crackers and a box of cheap supermarket brand teabags. No body parts. No severed heads waiting for me to discover. I moved on to the kitchen drawers next, which were filled with all sorts of assorted crap and unpaid bills. There was a pan on the stove with a few crusty beans in it spotted with green and white furry mould. Carrier bags filled with empty microwave meal boxes and takeaway cartons littered every surface, the handles tied into precise knots. I was again struck with a sense of a lonely existence. It was everywhere, and even as experienced as I was, it was a hell of an unsettling experience. I had spotted some loose papers on the side, and almost walked past the fridge when something caught my eye. I ducked into the alcove, unsure of what to expect as I reached out to the grimy, grease covered handle to see what might be inside. I froze when I saw the photo on the door. It was held in place by those colourful magnets shaped like letters of the alphabet, reminding me of my school days. My heart was slamming against my ribcage as I tried to take it all in. He must have known I was coming. He must have left this for me.

The photograph was a Polaroid taken with one of those old instamatic cameras. It was held in place by five magnets, the taunt clear and definitely meant for me to find.

SEE at the top of the picture and ME at the bottom, holding it in place. I didn't want to touch it, not until forensics had been in and swept the scene, and I didn't have to. The content of the picture was clear enough. We had all seen it just a few days ago. It was taken in the hotel room, and showed the butchered remains of the poor girl that started this whole saga.

"Perkins!" I yelled, unable to take my eyes away from the image.

I heard him come, asking what was wrong, but he sounded distant and might as well have been on another planet. All I could do was stare at the photograph. Until that point, all I could think about was finding Damon Benton and bringing him in. It was now, as I looked at his handiwork, I realised just how unstable the man was. It was then that I began to hope that I would be able to find him, before he found me.

"Christ," Perkins said as he stood beside me. "I'd better call this in."

I nodded. It was the best I could do. He was playing a game; that much was obvious. And as much as I knew I shouldn't, I was willing to go along with it in order to take him down, one way or the other.

* * *

I hung around for a time whilst forensics came in and did their thing. Although there didn't appear to be any other evidence apart from the picture, that was enough in itself. We also had those unpaid bills which we hoped might lead us to him, although I wasn't expecting them to come back with anything other than dead ends and false names. Sick of getting in the way, I headed back to the station, deciding it was a good idea to update Patterson on what was going on. I rang him on my way back, and he told me he had just stepped out, but was also on his way back, and I should meet him there. Apparently, they had solid info on a place of work for Benton, and Patterson was pouring all resources into this investigation. I was grateful. I wanted this prick caught, and fast. If only to get my life back.

I fought my way through the rabble and scum in the waiting room and headed upstairs. My head pounding, the stress beginning to wear me down. I just wanted a break, a chance to rest and forget about this shitty situation. I walked into the office, which was blessedly quiet and empty and I…

There was a box on my desk.

I stole a quick glance around the room, but there was no sign of anyone. Everyone was out and working. I knew it was from Benton. I just knew it. The style of the packaging was the same. So was the way it was addressed personally to me.

That little voice inside my head, the one I usually ignored and ended up regretting later, was screaming at me just to leave it, that it could be a bomb or anything, but I didn't think he would do that. Not since he seemed so keen on involving me in his little games. Ignoring the pleas of my inner voice, I lifted the lid off the box and looked inside.

I don't know if it was because I was half-expecting something awful, or because I was becoming desensitised to the constant horrors, but I barely flinched as I looked inside, even if my gag reflex almost made me puke all over what was undoubtedly evidence. I wondered if this was her, the girl he mentioned when he spoke to me on the phone. Or, more specifically, if it was part of her.

It was a severed head, the flabby fan of flesh where her chins would have been telling me she was a larger woman. Her eyes were missing, as were her ears. I couldn't see into her mouth, but I knew her tongue was gone too. There was that awful, sweet-sour stench of flesh just as it begins to turn, and as my stomach wavered in protest, I was grateful again that I hadn't eaten anything yet. I didn't want to touch the card that was in the box, and I hadn't had to. I was able to read it well enough from where I was standing.

See no evil.

Speak no evil.

Hear no evil.

It was another taunt, another test. He was getting more and more confident, and right then I'd known that forensics wouldn't find anything else at the flat. We'd only found the picture because he'd left it out to find. It was too much to hope that he'd be sloppy enough to leave anything else he didn't want found.

I flopped down in my chair, my legs feeling rubbery and unable to take my weight.

I don't know when Patterson had arrived. I heard him talking to me and the commotion as he'd seen the box and its contents, but even when the room had started to fill with people, I'd still not really been with it. I must have shut down for a while - maybe my overworked brain had wanted a break from the strain or something, but I hadn't had the power to stop it even if I'd wanted to. As stubborn and independent as I was, I was only human, and at that point in time, my ability to cope had been reduced to zero. I could hear Patterson saying something about where Benton worked, but none of it went in. All I did was stare at the box on my desk and wondered what I ever did to get the attention of this nut-job, and more importantly, how to put it right.

MONDAY

20.

I walked around the house with a feeling of confidence. The gallery was taking shape, it's ambience tainted only by the unusual scent of the dead; a smell I couldn't decide whether I liked or not. Despite my excitement about what was happening around me, I felt tired this morning. No doubt this was a result of being up all night, alternately working and letting myself go with my new-found sexual urges. I had to say – now that I realised they were a part of who I was - I'm kind of enjoying them. Guess I have Detective Andrews to thank for the sudden ability not to stress about them being wrong or bad form. Still, I had no time to think about the detective, or the urges, now. Time was ticking on and, more importantly, flesh was starting to rot.

Not that I minded too much. After all rotting flesh could symbolise the decay of society but, at the same time, I kind of wanted some of my pieces looking a little fresher for when I had the grand opening. Shame I wouldn't be able to get hold of the bits needed to embalm them. Given that the gallery didn't hold such items and, working there, I'd have no reason to own them, I couldn't help but feel it might have raised a few questions as to why the fluids were needed. Again, not important. Time was getting on and there was still a fair bit to be done.

Today's to-do-list included finishing off the art pieces I'd already started and then popping out for fresh supplies, but not before quickly checking the news channels just to see if I was a wanted man yet. If not now it would be happening soon - especially after I'd heard him say my name whilst on the telephone. If he hasn't already gone there, he would soon be heading to my apartment where he'd find that photograph I'd left for him.

Thinking about myself on the news programs, and in the papers, was scary. On the one hand it will be great to see my face in the media, and even greater to know that the detective hadn't been able to stop me from becoming famous, but on the other hand it would have been useful to remain anonymous for a little while longer. Not entirely necessary – would just be nice. If the worst case scenario did happen and they did pull me in, at least the house was more or less ready for some guests. It's just that the perfectionist dwelling in me, alongside the darkness, wanted to fill every room and see the whole plan through to the end. That same perfectionist wanted to really give them a gallery to appreciate and make the most of all potential opportunities for fame. Wouldn't want to disappoint them.

In the main room I turned my parent's old television set on. The amount of times I'd come back to this old house over the months, every time I was half-expecting to find someone had broken in and taken it. Each visit I'd been surprised to see that it was still here. Everything they'd left - well, *I* had left - was still here. A house frozen in time. As the months had gone by and the dust had begun to settle, I had to confess that it was getting a little creepy in here, especially with the ghosts of my parents roaming my mind, taunting me. The ghosts were all but gone, thanks to my mind being pre-occupied with thoughts of what I needed to do and thoughts of what I'd already done.

And even if the ghosts had still been present - it would have been harder to hear my parents' poisonous whispers telling me that I was nothing more than a failure and that I would never amount to anything when, over the past week, I'd achieved so much.

A week? Jesus. Time sure did fly when you're having fun.

I'd spent the next couple of idle hours hopping from channel to channel. Thankfully, none of them showed my face yet. Nothing saying anyone was looking for me. I felt a little deflated but then it could be that they were still trying to get an image of me. It's not as though I'd left one in the apartment. They'd be able to get one from the gallery, but that was a question of whether they'd even found out about where I'd once worked. Not being a police officer, or having a clue as to how things worked there, I wasn't entirely sure how long it would take to run a complete background check on someone. My previous experience of background checks, when I started new jobs, usually hinted that it took a while but no doubt the police could fast track it when they really needed to. Not that the background check would reveal much. Only that the name registered to that apartment was fake, my place of work and some old credit cards which I didn't really use that often. I turned the television off and tried to lift my spirits. It's good that I wasn't on the news yet. It meant I had a little longer to go unnoticed amongst the crowds. It's good, all good. Stop thinking about missed opportunities for fame – it would come as soon as we went 'live'.

* * *

I threw some clean clothes on – yesterday's clothes were tainted with bloodstains and bits of intestine - and grabbed the van keys from the hook next to the front door. A quick glance over my shoulder to see if I'd forgotten anything. Think I'm good. Opening the door I'd squinted as the brilliant sunlight had taken me by surprise. Okay, hadn't expected that. Thank God there was still a chill in the air. Didn't need it getting any warmer. After all, the warmer it was the faster my bodies would rot. Couldn't have that.

I stepped out of the house, closing the door behind me - but not before I gave my front pocket a gentle pat to ensure I'd remembered to pick my wallet up. Same credit cards I'd used yesterday. No need to get rid of them yet, as they couldn't be linked to a crime. Confident I had everything I needed, I hurried to the van and hopped into the driver's seat, sliding the key into the ignition and firing the engine up with a feeble splutter. Damn hire vehicle - wonder how often they serviced them? Slipping the gear stick into reverse I backed out of the driveway, careful to avoid the whale's broken heap and my own personal car as I did so. It didn't matter if the hire vehicle was dying a slow vehicular death. Only needed the van to last me a couple more days and even then I didn't need to do a lot of driving - so long as I found what I was looking for quickly. And, when I was ready to resume looking for subjects, I was sure a quick search in the red-light district would bear fruit. After that, whether the engine lasted or not, it really wasn't my concern.

Okay, first stop - I needed a stationery store. Thankfully there was a small one in the nearest village. A small, family-run affair. It should have the bits I was looking for; A4 card, some clip frames and black magic markers. Nothing too unusual or hard to source. Should have remembered those bits on Friday. And here I was thinking I'd been organised. Just goes to show - you never could plan enough. Probably would have been worth making notes as I'd gone along rather than being reliant on my memory. But then, notes equalled paper trail.

Ten minutes after leaving the house I'd arrived at the stationery store, abandoning the van by the curb-side. Minimum hassle. Just the way I liked it. Quaint little store. It never used to open on a Monday, but hard times, and customer demand, forced it to do so. The owners had made a fuss and said it would only be for the summer months but, not surprisingly, the summer months had soon turned to forever.

I jumped from the van and walked through the front door. A small bell above the door-frame signalled my entrance, followed seconds later by a plump girl coming from out the back of the shop. In my mind I was envisioning her having a small television set out there or, at the very least, some magazines to idly thumb through whilst passing the slow hours of the day.

"Afternoon," she said.

As soon as I'd seen her I'd forgotten my original purpose for visiting the store. My mind, transfixed by her looks, immediately threw a scenario into my consciousness, just from the sight of her alone. I smiled and wished her a good afternoon in return before turning my attention to the items of stationery I needed.

"At least the sun is shining today," she said referring to the weather. "I thought it was never going to stop raining." She must have been bored. Probably saw me as an easy way to kill a couple of tedious minutes.

I grabbed a handful of white A4 card from near the counter and placed it next to the till point. I smiled at her again, acknowledging what she was saying. She was a pretty woman - late twenties, possibly early thirties maybe? Plump but not like the whale. She had been fat in an unhealthy way. This lady was definitely smaller. Thank the lord. Not sure I would have been able to lift another beast - my back had barely survived the last one.

It was the shop assistant's plumpness which had attracted my attention when I'd first laid eyes upon her. It was her shape which had piqued my interest and had planted the idea of a new, surprising, scenario - a humorous one to lend some comedy to the proceedings. At least one which could help with an insanity plea if they weren't already convinced of it. Whatever. All I knew was that I wanted her. I needed her.

"Clip frames?" I asked.

She points across the store to the far wall where there were frames piled on top of each other. Some fancy looking and some like the basic glass clip-frames I was looking for. I nodded a thank you to her and went to fetch some. As much I had liked the expensive wooden ones, I thought it would be overkill for what I needed. Besides they only had one of them and I needed... what? Mentally counting up, I calculated I needed three. I picked up four - better safe than sorry - and went back to the counter where they were rung through the till.

"Anything else I can help you with?" she asked.

I turned my attention to the pots of pens - each type in their own individual tray in front of where I stood. I grabbed a couple of the medium-tipped black markers, putting them on the pile of goods I'd already chosen. I looked at the shop assistant and smiled - the best smile my mask allowed. Couldn't let her see what was thinking.

"Just one more thing," I said, a quick casual glance down to her hands. Fingers specifically. No rings. Always a bonus.

"Oh?"

"Your phone number..?" I said, flashing her another smile. It had been a long time since I had tried something like this and, even then, the last time hadn't been the success I'd wanted. Whatever her answer was to be, she at least blushed a little.

MONDAY

21.

I couldn't help laughing to myself while I dragged the body of the plump shop assistant into the house, hours after our initial encounter. What I had in mind for her was still causing me some amusement. I was just hoping that others would be as tickled by it as much as I was. Not that it mattered either way as, with her addition, I reckoned I finally had enough pieces to make the gallery work. Just needed to get them displayed to the same standard I'd set for the rest of my work and then I needed to secure Detective Andrews himself for, without him, my work wouldn't have as much of an impact.

The girl's body had dropped to the floor with a satisfying thump. Here would do. I'd set her up here. The first one they'd all see coming into the gallery. As I was admiring her cooling corpse I couldn't help wondering whether she was now in heaven wishing she'd given me her phone number instead of denying it, or perhaps wondering whether things would have worked out differently for her. I wasn't sure if it would have been any consolation for her to know that things would have been a little different but not terribly so. I supposed the main difference was that that I wouldn't have had to follow her back to her home and I wouldn't have had to hit her with the handy brick I kept in the front of the hire van. Chances were we could have had a pleasant evening together.

And then I would have clubbed her to death.

Out of breath from the strain of dragging her body in from the van, I couldn't help slumping down next to where I'd dropped her. Just needed a couple of minutes to sort myself out, catch my breath, and then I could get on with turning her into an amusing sculpture. I chuckled again as the idea popped back into my mind once more. I have to say, when I first started this hobby, I hadn't been sure how easy it was going to be. I hadn't been sure how I'd think up all the different pieces I wanted to create but... yeah... it had been pretty easy going. And to think, my so-called-father used to struggle to create new pieces of art.

Yeah, dad, who's the failure now? I thought, a smug grin spreading across my tired face.

Another minute had passed by. I could have stayed where I was, leaning against the wall, next to the body, for much longer, possibly even for the rest of the night, but there was too much work to be done so I forced myself up onto my aching feet and went into the kitchen where I'd stashed my tools.

From under the sink, I retrieved the small leather bag I needed, before returning to the little plump girl who was already stinking. I would need supports for this model, some wires strung from the ceiling to keep her in a standing position. I would also need... going into the small bag, I fished out a Stanley knife. Pushing the safety mechanism, the sharp blade slid out from the handle. I grinned at the sound of the blade revealing itself. Love that noise. Where was I? Oh yes. I would also need to gut her. Couldn't have anything in the stomach for this piece.

I pushed the blade down hard upon her flesh until it disappeared into her stomach then slid it the length of her gut. I pulled the blade out and dropped it as soon I felt the old familiar stirrings from below. For a split second I panicked, knowing what was coming, but then I calmed myself down.

It didn't matter.

Whatever it was I did, it didn't matter.

Just go with it.

Enjoy it.

Embrace it.

It's a part of who I am.

It had just revealed itself recently.

That was all.

Nothing more and nothing less.

Certainly nothing to panic about.

I hadn't even finished my internal pep-talk before I realised I'd unbuttoned the flies of my trousers. Seconds later, my erection was free. I heard my own voice telling me to enjoy it and embrace it and that, at this late stage of the game, it was okay.

I couldn't help thinking of Detective Andrews as I slid myself into the gash I'd made. The cool feeling of the girl's internal organs lubricating my penis. Good. Saves it from getting friction burns. I unconsciously muttered my thanks to Detective Andrews as I began thrusting in and out of the girl's body - her fat stomach wobbling with each motion. Thank you for having given me the determination not to let these actions bother me anymore. Thank you for having made me see the bigger picture. And thank you for having made me realise this is the person I am - killer, pervert, artist.

Gathering momentum I sighed. Who would have thought that this would feel so good? I repositioned myself so I could squeeze her sides in to make for a tighter fuck hole. A funny squelching sound echoed from the wound and through the hallway as I felt her internal organs tighten around the head of my cock. A pleasant feeling as I throbbed harder. Thoughts of cutting the whale's head off, rimming the school girl's empty eye-sockets, bathing in the whore's organs as they spilled over me once I sliced her stomach open, so many thoughts dancing through my mind. And the skin: the thought of the blade slicing the skin messily from the body of both the whale and the school girl... So vivid. So pretty. As pretty as the models looked after their displays had been completed.

And then it started to hit me, the familiar tingling spreading down my thighs. The orgasm shot through and out of me into the corpse's stomach. The mess didn't matter. It would soon come out, along with the rest of her innards. I breathed a heavy sigh of pleasure.

"Thank you Detective Andrews!" I said out loud, withdrawing my penis, a string of stomach lining catching on the end of it. Must have got tangled with all the thrusting. No matter, I wiped it clean with my own top. There was no issue with my clothes being bloodied once again - just as previous clothing had been dirtied on other nights working on my other sculptures. It wasn't as if they wouldn't have got messy anyway... but the rush of the orgasm had been worth it. I found myself laughing as I adjusted myself - returned my penis into my pants and did up my flies. So totally worth it and now that that was out of the way, I could continue with what needed to be done. I began by sticking my hand into that very same hole I'd just fucked, grabbing whatever I could and pulling my hand out - a handful of... I don't know what... coming out in my firm grip; some of which was coated in semen.

I threw the sticky mess to the floor and was instantly shocked to discover just how far the splatter radius spread. Couldn't leave it there. I would have to clean it up before guests could come over. It's so sticky, so messy... Definitely a slipping hazard...

Throwing another pile of internal mush in same place, I thought how it would have been a smart idea to put some sheeting down first. So many bodies in and yet I still had much to learn. What with model-making and clean up duty - it was going to be a long night.

TUESDAY

22.

Patterson had made me go home after the incident with the box, and told me to take Monday off as well. I wanted to work, but he hadn't given me a choice. Said I needed the rest. Fat chance of that happening. The clock told me its 1:44am, so that means it's technically Tuesday morning, although to me it's still Monday as I haven't slept yet. The house felt so empty without Lucy. At least I knew she'd got to her sister's in one piece. Wyatt checked in to let me know all had gone well, so that at least was one worry off my mind. Still, here I sat, three quarters of the way through a bottle of Jack Daniels and almost a full twenty-pack of fags smoked.

So much for willpower.

Still, even though this insomnia was kicking my arse, there were a few positives. Despite the care he thought he'd taken, we managed to get some more on Benton. Turns out the prick worked at the art gallery. We'd managed to pull his records and even a photo from when he'd had to have his I.D card made up. I had that fuzzy printout of his face right here. Not for the first time tonight, I held it up in front of me and stared into those shadowy eyes. Photograph or not, I almost felt him staring back at me. Some people say that you can always see it in the eyes, you know, whatever it is that makes killers kill, crazy people crazy, and nutcases nutty. I had always agreed with that in some respects, but as I looked at that photograph, I wasn't able to detect anything. Nothing at all. No humanity. No compassion. The eyes were as dead and lifeless as the paper they'd been printed on.

Realising my thoughts were a little too coherent, I'd taken another slug of my sour mash friend, enjoying the burn as I impatiently waited for it to make me too drunk to care about the world for a while.

First thing tomorrow, I'd head over to the art gallery. I knew he wouldn't be there, but the people he worked with could be our best shot at finding out exactly who he is and give us a little insight into the man behind this persona.

In hindsight, we should have checked the art galleries first. This guy obviously had an eye for drama, for making visual statements. As I sluggishly lit up another cigarette, I thought about how different things would have been if we'd only understood sooner where we should have been looking. The other thing that bothered me was where he was committing his murders. Forensics failed to find anything at the flat, so I could only guess that he had another place which he called home, somewhere private and quiet where he'd be undisturbed. Maybe a family home?

My heart beat a little faster at this possible lead, and although I considered it, I decided that ringing Patterson at almost two in the morning when blind drunk probably wouldn't do me any favours. Instead, I fished a pen out of my jacket pocket, and scrawled on the bottom of the photograph of Benton Family home???

That was about all that my alcohol-ravaged body had been willing to let me do, so I let both pen and printout fall to the floor as I took another slug of JD. I felt tired now, and my eyes were getting heavy. I half considered phoning Lucy but suspected that she would appreciate my drunken ramblings even less than Patterson would. Besides, I didn't know what I'd say to her anyway. My every movement felt as if I was underwater; slow and ponderous. It appeared to take an age to lift the bottle to my mouth. I spilled some of the booze down my chin, but by that stage I hadn't really cared. I was tired. So tired. I was thinking that maybe I should close my eyes, just for a second to get rid of the headache. Just a quick snooze maybe…

I heard the distant sound of the bottle falling onto the floor, then, blessed unconsciousness found me.

TUESDAY

23.

"Jesus, you look like shit, Martin," Perkins said with what I thought was great glee as I'd clambered into the passenger seat and pulled on my seatbelt.

"Piss off and drive, Perkins," I grumbled.

I suppose I couldn't complain. The hornet-like buzzing of my headache seemed to be my body's way of chastising me for the abuse I'd given it the night before. To say I felt rough was a huge understatement. Still, the constant throbbing in my skull didn't look like it was about to cease and so, partly out of need and partly to try and get one over on my pissed off body, I pulled out my last few fags and lit one up. Fuck you, lungs.

"Rough night?" Perkins asked, negotiating the early morning gridlock.

"Could say that," I replied while rubbing my temples.

"I thought you'd quit the ciggies?"

"I decided to start again, just for a while."

"Don't let that Mrs of yours find out, she'll kick your arse."

"She won't find out, I'll stop as soon as she gets back."

"You heard anything from her?"

"Yeah," I said with a sigh, hoping Perkins would get the hint and just stop talking to me. "Had a voicemail from her yesterday morning. Must have missed her call."

"I thought you'd told her not to ring until this was all sorted out?"

I rolled my eyes and even managed a smile. "You can tell you're single, Perkins. I haven't met a woman yet who does anything other than what they want."

There was silence for a while, apart from the steady pulsing in my head. Maybe, just maybe I was getting too old for this. As if voicing its agreement, my body turned up the headache intensity to 11.

Great.

"Do you expect to find anything here?"

"Probably not," I sighed, wincing at the clock and seeing that it wasn't even 9AM yet. "But the prick worked here for a while. Surely someone must have some kind of information on him. Anything that might give us a sniff of a lead. As careful as he's been so far, it'll only take one little slip up and I'll have him."

We pulled up at traffic lights next to a bus, the growling engine not helping my headache.

"Why do you think he chose you?"

I glanced over at Perkins, and saw him watching me. It took a while to figure out the expression on his face, and when it did finally hit me, I wished it hadn't.

He was looking at me like I was a dead man walking.

"Because, Perkins, you will learn as you do this job that every once in a while, a sick, twisted fuck like this will crawl out of the woodwork and want to make a name for himself. He sees all of these films, the big Hollywood blockbusters, right, with the overpaid actors with their perfect smiles playing detective as the killer stalks them. Our loner, he wants some of that. He wants the Hollywood sizzle, he wants the fame, the fortune and the glory. What he…."

A cyclist darted between us and the bus, clipping the wing mirror and making my heart almost leap into my throat. Christ, I was getting jumpy.

"Fucking idiot! Watch where you're going you stupid bastard!" I glared at him as he went, a blur of yellow hi-visibility jacket as he weaved through the gridlock. Twat. I got my thoughts back on track and turned back to Perkins. "As I was saying, this dickhead wants the fame and the fortune. He wants the spotlight. What he doesn't seem to grasp is that real life isn't nearly half as interesting as Hollywood, and I'm no George Clooney or that other prick, the one who was in Batman."

"Michael Keaton?"

"No, the new one."

"Christian Bale?"

I nodded, "Yeah, that's him. I don't know if our killer sees me as his great nemesis, and I don't know, if he does, why he thinks that. But either way, it is what it is and until he's caught, I just have to live with it. Take this advice Perkins. Never let shit like this break you from your daily routine. If you do that, they win. I hope you never have to go up against anything like this, but it would be good advice to keep in mind if it should crop up in the future."

Although it wasn't my intention, but also not entirely unwelcome, the conversation was effectively killed at that point, and the rest of the slow drive to the art gallery was mostly undertaken in blessed silence.

We arrived just as the gallery was opening, meaning it was serene and quiet. The building manager was a sour faced, unsmiling bulldog of a man who didn't even recognise Benton when I showed him his photograph. He suggested we speak instead to his direct superior, a nice old guy called Gary. You could tell he was one of those people who didn't get into trouble. He was giving us that wide-eyed, fearful stare as we sat him down in the staffroom to question him.

"How long have you known Mr Benton?" I asked, watching for those tell-tale signs of a lie in his reactions.

"Pretty much since he started. He's a nice chap. A bit quiet, but polite."

"When did you last speak to him?"

"Last Thursday I think. That's right. He was off sick during the week and I asked him if he wanted to come over for dinner one night. Takeaway, of course. Wouldn't want to inflict my wife's cooking on anyone."

"Did he seem different to you at all?" I asked, rapidly losing faith that we would find anything here to lead us to this bastard.

"No, not in the least…. Is he in some kind of trouble?"

I flashed a quick look to Perkins. "We just want his help with our enquiries. We need to speak to him urgently."

"Oh, well I'm afraid nobody can reach him. He hasn't been in for a few days now. We tried calling him, but he doesn't answer the phone. It doesn't even ring anymore, so it must be switched off or something. I really don't have anything else to tell you."

I sat back in my chair, unsure of what I should do next. It seemed Benton was as anonymous at work as he was in the rest of his life, and tracking him down was going to be harder than I thought.

"Does he have a locker?" Perkins asked.

I looked at Perkins, and could have kissed his head. I don't know how I'd missed it. The far wall was lined with staff lockers for their personal belongings.

"Yes," the old man said, rummaging in his pocket. "I have the master key here."

This could be it, our breakthrough. The old man crossed the room and unlocked the one in the corner, standing back afterwards. I opened it, half wondering if he might have guessed this course of action and left me another one of his gruesome packages, but there was nothing there that was out of the ordinary. A spare shirt crumpled in the corner. A few CDs and a half-eaten pack of mints. It was then that I saw it, the chink in his armour, the one thing that he might well have forgotten.

A photograph, taped to the inside of his locker door showing was a large, private house, set in its own lands. Although the image was faded and yellowed, I couldn't help thinking that, as a location, it would be the perfect place for him to commit his atrocities.

I snatched the photograph from the locker and showed it to Gary.

"Any idea where this is?"

"No, I'm sorry, I've never seen it before."

I nodded and gave the picture to Perkins, "Get that to the nerds back at the station. I want to know where it is, and I want to know now. Also, take his mug-shot from the employee records and get copies of it made. Lots of them."

"Why?"

"Because we're going to go public and put this prick on the front of every newspaper in the country. If he's out there, someone will know about it."

"Isn't that what he wants?"

"We won't mention the crimes. Just say he's wanted for questioning. Blame terrorism if you have to, anything but the real reason. Get on it right now. I'll clear it with Patterson."

As Perkins scurried away, for the first time I felt like I could be at least be on level terms with this dickhead instead of two steps behind. He claims to want the fame. Let's see if that really is the case.

WEDNESDAY

24.

My face is in the news now. Thank God. I'd been irritated yesterday when I hadn't been able to find myself on any of the news programs. Nor had I found myself in the daily newspapers - not even a hint of my existence - when I'd popped to the village newsagent to grab a fresh pint of milk. Mind you, irritated as I was, I couldn't help laughing when I saw people banging on the door of the stationery store trying to get someone to open up for them. Wonder how long they'd waited. Other than that, Tuesday had been nothing more than a wasted day of channel-hopping and quiet seething. But now, this morning, it's all but forgotten thanks to seeing a picture of my handsome self on the morning news show. I knew it wouldn't be long as I could tell, instantly, that they had got the picture from the gallery where I worked. Must have picked it up yesterday.

With regards to the news report, they hadn't said why I was wanted for questioning which was a bit of a disappointment. They just reported that the police were keen to speak to me and that anyone with information of my whereabouts should contact them immediately but in no way attempt to get in my way. In the great scheme of things it didn't matter though. The fact they were willing to report about me in the first place... Well, that just meant they'd be willing to write my story when I invited them to. And speaking of which, I'm ready - the final touches were put on some of the pieces yesterday and the others were still holding together well enough on their own, despite the speed with which they're decomposing.

The rest of my day would be spent phoning up the various companies who broadcast the news. I didn't need to go crazy. The local news stations and the local papers would be enough. Once they had the story… well, the rest of the world would pick it up from them, along with any images they'd captured on their private walk around.

The plan was simple. Put together late last night whilst attempting to distract myself from the irritation of not being in the spotlight. I'd waited for recognition - recognition which had come today – and now I would phone the news stations and local presses and inform them of what was in store for them. I'd tell them about the body the police had kept from them and that there were more waiting to be discovered in my beautiful gallery. I'd take a direct number for their chief reporter and leave them with the knowledge that I would be calling first thing Thursday morning and that, when I did, they would have to head to the address I gave them immediately or else miss the chance for the story of the century. And then, Thursday morning, I'd phone Detective Andrews and I'd tell him that I'm ready to give myself up. No doubt he'll invite me to the station but that's not how it will work. If he wants me then he has to come here and get me.

Because of what I've done, I know he won't come alone. I know he'll bring people with him but that won't matter. I say the more the merrier. I'm not shy. Hell, if I'd had more time, I'd try and invite even more people to come down here and see my work first hand but, alas, time is limited, what with the speed my sculptures are decomposing (the schoolgirl stinking the worst so far).

Art

I started to drift off back into my own little world, once more thinking about the dream I'd had after returning from the hotel. The flashing lights, the people here to see me, the crowds calling my name and surging forward to try and get a piece of me. Me just standing there with my arms outstretched as though wanting to pick everyone up in the crowd; bringing them into my inner circle.

I couldn't help smiling as I slowly returned to the present day.

It was all quite exciting really, certainly enough to cause some butterflies in my stomach. I felt like a young child at Christmas time, once they'd spotted the parcels left under the tree by the big man in the red suit. Another candidate for a police-led investigation into a paedophile on the loose for sure. There are some sick people in the world. Forget about them. It's not about them it's about me. It's all about me. My time has come. My time to shine and I will not let them ruin it for me - even though a brief thought popped into my mind pointing out that someone worse than I was could be just around the corner. After all, as I kept telling myself, society is sick. No, forget about them. Keep reminding yourself that this is your time. Do not fall apart now. Don't lose confidence in your work. You'll be remembered.

You'll amount to nothing, whispered the voice of my father.

"I *will* amount to something. You're just jealous that no one remembers you or your work. People will remember both my art and the person who created it. My art will make me immortal. Up there with the greats."

No one will remember you. No one will care for you. My mother's loving input.

I push their words out of my mind. I knew it wasn't really them, it's just me taunting myself, doubting myself as I get to the final chapter of my project. All great artists have moments of self-doubt. This just proved to me that I was up there with the best of them. This was my moment of crisis. I would overcome it just as the other greats had.

I ran from the lounge, where the television was still flickering in the corner of the room, and into the hallway where I picked up the old telephone from the small cabinet by the front door. Mum had liked it there. She would sit on the bottom stair for hours, yakking away to her friends. At least I always believed they'd been her friends but, as the years had gone on, I'd come to realise she'd been on the phone to the doctors talking about my father and his antics. Push the memory away, it wasn't important.

Relief flowed through me then as I heard the dial tone singing down my ear. A stroke of luck considering I hadn't checked it earlier. It was an old phone, so I wouldn't have been surprised if it hadn't worked properly. I froze as I suddenly realised I had no idea how to go about getting the numbers I so desperately sought. Slowly I put the handset back on its hook. All the planning I'd done and this is what had stumped me?

Not my fault. Originally I'd planned to use the Polaroid's I'd taken of the whore as invitations which I was going to post out. It had been a late night decision that changed my mind; after finishing with the plump girl, I'd decided it wouldn't the best way of inviting people. They'd have received the invitations at different times, and possibly some of them would get lost in the post. Then some would have come here straight away too. No order. Just chaos. No, invitations definitely weren't the way to go. Besides which, I was reluctant to give away any photographs I'd taken. Perhaps if I'd made copies?

Not important, I told myself again. I was merely distracting myself with little things. Why? Was I trying subconsciously to delay proceedings on the off-chance I'd change my mind? Why would I do that? I chuckled as I realised I was doing it again.

I turned my attention back to the phone. How best was I to accomplish this?

Of course. There was there was a service available to people searching for the numbers of companies. So obvious. I'm just getting clumsy now, forgetful even. Trying to rush things. I shouldn't rush, it would lead to mistakes. Or *could* lead to mistakes I should say. I should take my time, and calm down. Putting the phone back onto its cradle I took several deep breaths. Come on. Stay calm. Stay in control. You've got this. Home stretch. Don't mess it up. You've got this. You've got all day to phone these people – just take five minutes to gather your thoughts. Calm yourself down so you sound professional on the phone. You've come so far. Don't let your standards slide now. You owe it to yourself.

You'll amount to nothing.

* * *

The toilet was filled with vomit and the bathroom, in turn, thick with its stench. The mirror, part of the medicine cabinet which hung on the wall, had been smashed to pieces and blood was trickling from my hands and splattering onto the floor. A frenzied loss of control, thankfully temporary, as the doubts continued to plague me, I felt the taunting of my mother and father playing in my mind.

I was calm now. Still shaking but calm. I felt stupid for the state I'd managed to work myself up to. There really hadn't been any need. I'd done so much. I'd achieved so much. I should be feeling proud. I shouldn't be feeling this doubt. It's that Detective Andrews' fault. That little cunt telling me he'd keep my art away from the press. The way he told me no one would remember me. The threat of keeping it all a secret. What if he did? That piece of shit. No. He can't. He can't stop it from coming out. No matter what he says. It will come to light. The way I'll be revealing my gallery - there's no way it couldn't come to light. But society is sick - sicker than this perhaps. What if they didn't care because they've seen worse? Or better, depending on your outlook?

I felt myself beginning to well up again as the doubt laid its foundations deep within. I shook it away. Couldn't let myself think like this. I just needed to get downstairs, then phone directory enquiries for the numbers I needed and talk to the press people. I just needed to get that little bit done and then - that's it, I could relax. It wouldn't matter if doubt set in then, it would be too late. No turning back.

I clambered to my feet from where I'd dropped to my knees next to the stained toilet. I caught sight of myself in one of the mirror's broken fragments. I looked like Hell. So, so stupid.

I kept enumerating all that I'd achieved and I was starting to perk myself up. At least I guess I was beginning to perk up for, running mentally through my achievements, I felt a stirring in my crotch.

There you go, I admonished, just do what needs to be done then perhaps take a little time out with some of the off-cuts. Give myself a little treat to relax into my last evening in this house. Enjoy myself. I deserved it.

I left the bathroom hoping that, in so doing, I'd be able to hear the positive side much clearer than if I'd stayed there being taunted by the broken mirror – the after-effects of my loss of my self-control. Out of sight, out of mind.

I'm sure I'll feel better once I'd make the phone calls. Any thoughts of a crisis of faith would soon be replaced with both a feeling of excitement and nervousness as the time got ever closer for my work to be revealed. Even then, with just that little thought popping into my mind, a tiny butterfly fluttered in my stomach. A strange sensation but one that was infinitely better than the despair and worthlessness I'd felt in the bathroom.

Get the calls done, I told myself, once more making my way across the hallway and down the stairs to the phone.

I kept playing through what I needed to say when I got through to the relevant people. I'd tell them about the police hiding news from them, and about the whore in the hotel room. I'd give them the name of the detective in charge of the case and would describe what I'd done to the schoolgirl's eyes and where I had sent them. I'd explain why I was doing it and how my works of art reflected the stinking rot of today's toxic society. I would keep talking for as long as they'd listen, revealing details of my gallery and what they could expect from it. About then, I'd offer them the chance to come down and take photographs for their papers. Let them know they'll be the first to see my art. No journalist would ever be able to resist that. And then, when they had been hooked in and wanted more, I'd ask for a mobile number so I could send the address and a warning that the police would soon be here so they may want to get here as quickly as possible. After all, it was hardly likely that they would be invited to stay once the police arrived.

Jesus - all of that sounded so easy in my mind and yet I knew, when it came time to speak to them, I'd get flustered. Possibly even stumble over one or two of my words like a bumbling idiot.

Try not to think about it, I told myself. The more I thought about fluffing my lines, the more likelihood there was of making a mistake and tripping over my words. The same with over-thinking what I had to say - that could only ever end badly too. Besides I was sure I'd still forget something I was supposed to say if I ended up trying to stick to an accurate script. I shook my head. I couldn't risk it. I had a rough idea of what to tell the people, and a rough plan of what to say. That should be enough. I was intelligent enough to just be able to respond to how they were on the phone.

I picked a newspaper up from where I'd thrown it onto the hallway floor during the week - something I often did once I'd finished reading it. Next I picked up the phone and sat myself down on the lower step of the stairs. Okay. Here we go. I took a deep breath. I'd start with the local press. They'd be the easy ones to get hold of - their phone numbers would be listed on the editorial pages. Start with the easy calls and then move onto the television stations - the ones which would take a little more research...

My hand was visibly shaking as I flicked to the contact section.

Another deep breath.

WEDNESDAY

25.

No sleep again. Every time I closed my eyes I'd see Benton's face, and every time I heard a noise in the house or outside, I was sure it would be him and had to get up to check. I hated the fact he'd managed to get inside my head so much. I could never let anyone know of course. I have an image to uphold. This house is a desolate and morose place without Lucy, so empty and quiet. It's odd how you take for granted having another person share your living space. Still, my routine went on. I washed, skipped shaving again, drank my morning coffee. I didn't eat because I had no appetite these days, however I smoked a couple of fags. Those things had crept back into my life with depressing ease, but I was determined to stamp them out again, just as soon as this situation had been dealt with.

At least today we might see something happening. The press would be plastering Benton's face all over the news this morning. I'm curious to see how he copes with all the added pressure and attention. My phone vibrated on the table beside me, and I picked it up to see who the text message was from.

About to go public with the photo. What is this all about???

It was from my friend, Alex. He was my go-to guy in the press if I needed to leak any information. We had known each other since school, and I trusted him completely. Still, I couldn't fill him in on this, not yet, and so I decided to do the one thing I was getting good at.

Nothing serious. Wanted for questioning, need to add pressure.

I pressed send and hoped he would leave it there, but like a dog chewing a bone, he didn't. His name flashed up on the display as he called me, and although I half-wanted to ignore it, I picked up and answered.

"Come on, Martin, don't give me the silent treatment. This is obviously something big, come on, give me something."

As always, he was right to the point, all business. I couldn't help but admire him, and thought that under different circumstances, he would have made a really good police officer.

"I can't give you any more than I already have. We just want him in for questioning, nothing else."

"Come on, you wouldn't go national with this unless it was something serious. Can't you give me something, just a sniff?"

"I can't, really. I'm sorry."

"Even off the record?"

Despite everything, I smiled. It was the first time in a while. I knew I shouldn't say anything, but I also knew I could trust Alex completely, and if he said it was off the record, then I was confident it would remain that way until I gave the nod to go public.

"You can't go public with this, not even hint at it. Understood?"

"You know me, I wouldn't fuck this up for you. Come on, spill it. What's the story with this Benton guy?"

"You better not, because you are literally the only person outside of the investigation who knows. I know I can trust you, but this is something big. Do you understand?"

"Yeah, of course. I won't breathe a word."

Despite being able to hear the excitement in his voice, I knew he could be trusted, and so I filled him in. He didn't interrupt or cut me off, he just listened and let me get it off my chest, which on its own felt good. When I'd finished, there was silence for a few seconds.

"Is Lucy okay?"

"Yeah, she's safe. I just want to nail this prick, Alex. It's all I think about."

"Are you sure you should be keeping this from the public? From what you said, this guy sounds like a fucking loon."

"Tell me about it, but that's what he wants. He craves the attention, he wants to be noticed. I'm not about to give him that satisfaction."

"Even if he kills again?"

I had considered that, and although it pained me to say what came next, I knew it was for the right reasons.

"Yeah, even if he kills again. Believe me, it sounds harsh but if this wanker gets the attention of the public, who knows how far he might go."

"But why the obsession with you? Where do you fit in?"

"Who knows? I think it was just because I was the first to question him about it. I left him my card and he must have decided that he wanted to involve me in his sick games."

"So what's the plan now?"

"Well, I'm hoping that once this goes national we might get a hit from the member of the public. A sighting or something. Of course, there will be all the shitty hoaxes and misinformation, but it will only take one lead to nail him."

"Well, for the record, I think you're doing the right thing by keeping a lid on it. Last thing you need is public hysteria whilst this guy goes around slicing people up. Is there anything I can do to help?"

"Just make sure that photograph gets circulated everywhere. The more pressure I can heap on this guy, the more chance I think he'll crack."

"Will do. If I hear anything at my end, I'll get straight in touch."

"I appreciate it, thanks Alex."

"Anytime... Hey Martin, you take care of yourself, okay? You don't sound too good."

That was an understatement. I felt like shit, but wasn't about to admit it. Not with that thing called pride getting in the way.

"I'm fine, really. Just want to get this resolved that's all. Thanks Alex, I appreciate the support."

"Anytime pal, I'll be in touch if anything crops up at my end."

The line went dead, and I shoved my phone in my pocket. It was time to head in to the office and see if there would be any movement. One thing I was certain of, is that life was about to become a little less easy for our would-be artist.

WEDNESDAY

26.

The station was a hive of activity when I arrived. Every major news and radio outlet was carrying Benton's image and description, and almost from the off the phones had been constantly ringing. Patterson looked flustered as I slipped my jacket off and hooked it over the back of my chair.

"Jesus Christ, Martin, I hope you know what you've started here. We can't keep up on the phones."

"Any solid leads?"

"Who knows, we're taking information down as it comes in, but the crazies have already started to call in with fucking stories about how Benton is an alien and stuck a probe up them. I swear I wonder about some people in this world."

I had to stifle a smile at my flustered boss. Like the rest of us, he wasn't used to such an intense work environment.

"Things will calm down, but to make things easier, I only want to see reports that took place within an initial 5 mile radius. I don't think he will have strayed too far. If we can prioritise those, Perkins and me will go through them and decide which ones to look into first."

"I don't know how you expect to dig any truth out of all these fucking crank calls. Talk about a needle in a haystack." He shook his head and shrugged.

In truth, I wasn't sure either. I was relying on something, some instinct to point me in the right direction. I was also relying on Benton too. I'm sure he wouldn't want to stay hidden from me for too long. And so, with quiet confidence, I retreated to my desk and started to sift through the incoming reports. Patterson was right about one thing: the crazies were really outdoing themselves.

Morning drifted into afternoon, and still the reports came in. We had fielded almost five hundred calls since the news broke, and although I had initially expected some kind of breakthrough, not a single lead looked to be panning out.

My phone started to ring, and I saw Alex's number flash up on the display.

"Hello?" I said as I lifted the handset to my ear.

"Hey, it's me. You weren't lying about the coverage. Every station is carrying this."

"That was the plan. What have you got for me?"

"Well, to be honest, I'm not sure. I've just had a call from a strange-sounding guy. Said he wanted to invite me to his gallery for a special exhibition."

It was him, I just knew it.

"Did he just send it to you?"

"No, everyone got it. Checked in with a few of my friends. The

Star, the Herald and the Express all received the same call. Could this be a copycat or something? An attention-seeker taking advantage of the hype?"

"No, it's impossible. Nobody knows about the art angle apart from us and you. You didn't tell anyone did you?"

"No, of course not. I thought you knew me better than that. I made a promise."

"Sorry, I just needed to check. Where is the exhibition?"

"He said to expect a text with the details first thing tomorrow morning. He hung up after that. Whatever you intended Martin, if this is your guy then he doesn't seem too bothered by the attention. What do you want me to do?"

"Sit on it for now. With luck, nobody will connect this with our killer, and so might not bother to show up tomorrow. As soon as you get an address, you tell me and only me. I want officers out to whatever location before the rest of the press can get there. Can I count on you?"

"Of course you can. Friends first, right?"

"Thanks Alex. No matter what time it is, you make sure you call me as soon as you get that address. I'll be here at the station waiting."

"Understood. I'll get back to you as soon as I get the info."

I hung up the phone and took a second to take it all in. I knew it was Benton. Could he be finished with his little game? Maybe now that he was in the media, it wasn't what he had expected and wanted it all to end? As much as that would be nice, I doubted that was the answer. It appeared to me that this had already gone too far for him to just give up.

Whatever he had planned, it seemed to that he wanted the world to see it, and that was something I didn't like one bit.

THURSDAY

27.

I wasn't able to sleep last night. The anticipation of today has been too much and my stomach had been doing turns all night, whilst mixed thoughts of excitement and self-doubt plagued my now-tired mind.

I'd lost count of the amount of times I'd walked around the house, making sure everything was as it should be with the sculptures. Each check revealed all to be well and yet, within five minutes of sitting back down, I'd find myself checking again despite telling myself not to be so stupid and reassuring my brain that it really wasn't necessary.

By the time the sun had punctured the night-time sky and cast light upon the fields at the back of the house, I was already dressed in my new suit, a tidy black number which fitted beautifully. It even had a waistcoat. A red tie wrapped around my neck with a loose knot. I went with red because it matched, in places, my sculptures. Nice to keep a colour theme going.

I'd wasted a couple more hours walking around the house pacing up and down, and making sure all was still well. It was. Ten minutes, if that, was used to pour champagne into plastic cups I'd picked up on one of my many shopping trips. Couldn't afford the luxury of crystal glasses. Not that it mattered. After all, I wouldn't be using the cups again (no matter what they were made of). The cups had then been put onto a large silver tray, an article I'd accidentally stumbled upon when last I was in town. I'd walked past a charity shop and there was the tray - sitting pretty in the store's window display. Less than five pounds later and it was mine.

I'd moved the tray, as well as the cups of bubbly, through to the hallway. That's where I'd be standing when the guests would arrive after all. That's where I'd be handing them out. Chances are I'll run out pretty early on so I must be sure to keep a cup for Detective Andrews - I wouldn't want him to feel unwelcome. I wouldn't want him to look grumpier than need be when it came time to take our pictures for the front pages - me in cuffs and him leading me away.

My heart skipped a beat at the mere thought of it. I'm not sure whether that was down to feeling nervous or excited. Maybe a little bit of both? Time will tell, I guess.

I turned my mobile phone on for the first time in as long as I could remember. Must have been three days since I'd last checked it. A couple more minutes were thankfully wasted as it slowly booted up and came to life. Instantly messages flashed up on the home screen warning me that I had new voice-mail messages. I'm not that desperate to waste time so I wasn't going to listen to them. Chances are it was only work anyway - no doubt trying to find out what had happened to me. They probably think I've died. Or at least had thought that, - before the papers released my photo. Pretty sure they'd now got the message that I wasn't be going back in.

For some reason my mind bounced back to thinking about Gary standing on some golf course somewhere, a nine-iron in his hand. Not sure what this feeling is that's bubbling inside of me all of a sudden?

Is it that I'm missing the senile old fart? I concentrated on the feeling. No. It was one of regret. I still quite liked the idea of recreating the tableau of the last supper with him and his wife - both face down in their bowls of soup.

Too late now.

The way my pieces are currently smelling - I couldn't delay the gallery by another day even if it meant the addition of another great piece of work. Maybe one day, if I ever get out of prison, I'll be able to recreate another gallery somewhere. Perhaps do it somewhere overseas? Be nice to get out of this damned cold weather... although, if I did end up doing that, I would definitely need to think about getting some air conditioning in to keep the pieces looking fresh for longer.

Jesus - getting ahead of myself. Haven't even seen the reaction to this gallery yet and already I'm thinking about a second one. Come on. Stop that. One thing at a time...

... And speaking of time.

It was nine o'clock.

The news offices would be open now.

It was time to send a text message or two...

With shaking digits, I hit the button which invited me to create a new text message. Once done I fished in my pocket for the piece of paper on which was written the mobile numbers of my guests. Six numbers in total. It didn't appear a lot but I knew it was more than enough to get the message out there. Everything else would be done via word of mouth and, thanks to technology, I was expecting it to reach across the seas within hours, if not sooner.

Another heart flutter.

Exciting times indeed.

I started inputting the numbers into the contact section whilst trying to ignore my fluttering heart. To think a couple of weeks ago I was a nobody but, by the end of the day I will be somebody. Somebody famous.

I paused, waiting for the voices of my parents to spoil my moment, but there was just silence. They remained quietly in their graves, where they belonged. I smiled. Still can't believe I got away with that one. Innocent face I guess - useful for when I told people I had nothing to do with it and it was purely an accident. Hell, from time to time I believe it myself. I didn't do it. It wasn't me. It was just dumb luck. I laughed again as I realised just how fortunate I'd been to get away with it and, more importantly - how easy I'd found it to believe in my own lies. Truly a master of deceit. I put the memory to the back of my mind. So easily denied until this slip up. Perhaps I'd come clean about that when the time was right but that time is not now. Before I knew what I was doing I had pressed send on the text.

And there it goes; the address of my gallery to a handful of journalists.

I wasn't going to phone Detective Andrews just yet. No need. I'll let the message get to the journalists first and then, after they'd arrived and had the chance for a look round... *then* I'll get in touch with him.

Allow the journalists maximum exposure to really let my work sink into their minds. And, better yet, give them the necessary time to ensure they get all the photographs they want before the police kick them out.

My phone pinged back a delivery report. All messages had been received. Another heart flutter. I smiled for no more than a second as a feeling of panic suddenly caught me by surprise. They'd received the text messages. That would means they're on their way. I need to make sure everything is perfect! I jumped to my feet, slid the mobile phone into my pocket and rushed up the stairs to where the sculptures were kept.

Oh God! I hope they're still okay!

* * *

By the time I'd finished checking the displays, for what felt like the hundredth time, vehicles were pulling up on the drive outside. My heart was beating hard and fast now; nerves, anticipation and excitement surging through me. I couldn't show I was nervous though. I couldn't even show I was excited. I needed to remain professional, I needed to look confident. A man in charge. I am a man in charge.

I positioned myself in the hallway next to the plump woman who I'd covered up with a white sheet. A little bit of gore had leaked through but it that didn't matter. People would be able to guess what was under there anyway and they'd get to see it themselves but only after Detective Andrews gets to see it. He was to be the first to lay his eyes on it and see the joke. I laughed at the thought of his facial expression and quickly pushed the image from my mind. Must stay professional.

I picked the tray of drinks up from the carpet next to the plump girl's feet and balanced it on my arm as though I was a professional waiter and then waited. And waited. I know they're here, I heard the cars outside. Why aren't they coming to the door? Why aren't they knocking so I can shout for them to enter? Is there a problem?

I waited a couple more minutes and eventually put the tray of drinks back on the floor. Counted down from ten - just to be sure - but still no one knocked, or rang the doorbell. Slowly I walked over and pulled on the handle, opening the door slowly. There were five, maybe six, cars. The drive was full. People were sitting inside, all of them looking just as nervous as I felt.

It was be expected I guess. None of them knew what to really expect. Hell some of them, when I'd talked to them, thought it was going to be nothing more than a prank. I assured them it wouldn't be and that they'd have to take my word for it or simply miss out on the story of their career. I knew they wouldn't be able to ignore that. At least I hoped that they wouldn't have been able to ignore it. Of course, I wouldn't have had the problem had I sent the paper invitations as originally planned. Another shake of my head to rid myself of another unwanted and unnecessary thought. They're here. It doesn't matter. They came.

I waved my arm, a gesture letting them know they'd found the right place. A gesture letting them know they were more than welcome to come in.

I saw them looking at each other as though they were reassuring one another that everything was okay and that they'd be perfectly safe. Stupid. Over-active imaginations. Of course they'd be okay. They were my chosen guests. I shouldn't have been surprised by their reaction though. After all, being journalists, they're probably used to seeing a whole manner of horrors on a day to day basis; wars, rapes, murders, thefts and, of course, political scandals. These people have seen it all. At least, they think they have. After today... after today they *would* have seen it all.

I flashed them a smile and waved them in again.

THURSDAY

28.

I'd spent the night at my desk. One by one people had gone home, until I was left in an empty office, staring at the same evidence which still hadn't given me anything new. I had gone beyond being tired, and had transcended to a place where I was running on willpower alone. Alex never called back. I tried him a few times, but after the first few calls rang unanswered, the phone stopped ringing at all. I presume the lure of whatever bait that Benton had dangled and the story that would follow was too much to resist. In a way, I couldn't blame him. If his colleagues were all going to be there, it seemed only fitting that he should be too. Still, I wasn't in the mood to fuck around, and if Benton got away, then I wouldn't hesitate to run Alex in for obstruction of justice or anything else I could get him on. This was bigger than careers and bigger than getting the next big scoop, this was about life and death. I had other contacts in the media of course but I'm sure word had already gone around to make sure the police were kept out of the loop until the press could get their pound of flesh.

As mid-morning approached, I was starting to think it might be an idea to go to the paper's offices and drag them all in for questioning, when my phone rang. The display said number withheld, and I knew, before I even answered it, who would be on the line.

With my stomach rolling, I pressed the answer key.

"Hello?"

"Good morning. That's a nicer greeting. Good morning. Because you're actually wishing the person on the end of the phone a good morning. So... did you want to try again? Did you want to wish me a good morning? Not that it really matters because, for what it's worth, I'm having an amazing morning. So many photographers here. So many camera flashes, both aimed towards my work and my own handsome face."

"What do you want?" I said, recognising that voice. The voice of the man I'd become obsessed with. He went on as if I hadn't even spoken.

"I won't lie, to start off with, I was a little uncomfortable about having my picture taken but, after a while, I got used to it. Now I just enjoy it. Never been good at pictures beforehand, you see. I feel as though I always looked a little rough but I've learnt that the trick to taking a good picture is remaining oblivious to the camera. Ignore it. Pretend it's not there. Act natural. No fake smile. No awkward, gimpish expression. Sure, some pictures not might be perfect but... Still better than if you try and pose for them."

I said nothing. I didn't want to give him the satisfaction. All I could do was grip the phone and grit my teeth to stop myself from losing it.

"Sorry, listen to me, I'm rattling on... that wasn't my intention. I just wanted to invite you down to my good morning. Feels strange celebrating this and yet not having you here. So... if you're interested, I'll pass on the address and you can come and meet us all. What do you say? Got a pen and paper? Good memory perhaps? The address is The Manor, Cutthroat Lane... quite apt don't you think? Well, would love to stay and chat but I really must dash. People are trying to talk to me and I fear I'm being rude to my fans. See you soon though, I hope?"

The line went dead, but I had scrawled the address on my pad and was already bringing up the internet. Bless Google and their invasive street view software. I punched in the address and waited for the slow as shit police internet to load my results. The image appeared on screen. I manipulated the mouse, and there it was. That same house from the photograph in his locker. Our own people were still working on tracing it, but it seemed that Benton had saved me the trouble. Whatever he was planning, he obviously wanted me to see, and if what he said was true, then it was already going on without me. I knew I should wait for Patterson and backup, but I was never the most patient. Instead I called him and explained, told him to get everyone out there as quickly as possible. For good measure I told dispatch to get all available units to the scene. I was done waiting. I was done with all the stupid little cat and mouse games. If Benton wanted me there, then I was going to oblige. I shrugged into my jacket, fished out my car keys and raced out of the building.

THURSDAY

29.

The police had taken even less time than I'd imagined to get to the property but that wasn't the end of the world. I had still given the guests enough time to get the photographs they'd wanted to take (reluctantly by the sounds of some of the mutterings I'd heard from upstairs) and by the time I heard the sirens coming most appeared to have even been done with the whole gallery. A look of horror on their faces which suggested to me that they wouldn't forget what they'd seen or the person who'd created the masterpieces. Some of them even had sick on their chins after they must have been ill. Hope they managed to keep it off of the sculptures.

I couldn't do anything but stand there and smile despite the questions being thrown at me by those who weren't in a corner vomiting.

Why did you do it?

Are they real?

What kind of monster would do such a thing?

Of course I ignored all of the questions. It wasn't their business. Not yet. Not before Detective Andrews got here and asked me himself. He's the officer in charge. He's the one who would get to ask the questions. No one else would do. Speaking of which...

... the sirens are right outside.

This is it.

Doors are slamming shut.

I could hear voices. They sounded urgent. Perhaps orders being issued? Not quite shouting but at the same time not quite whispers either. Not sure why - surely if they'd wanted this to be a surprise attack they would have killed the sirens long before showing up on the driveway? Sure they have their reasons.

Footsteps approaching the door.

The door suddenly flew open, helped by the foot of an overly keen uniformed officer. I didn't jump. I expected as much from them. I was just standing there with the tray of remaining drinks in my hand.

Officers spilled into the house.

Guns pointing at me.

Talk about bringing in the heavy hitters.

How exciting.

"Damon Benton?" one voice shouted.

"My name is Arthur," I said to the line of gun barrels, "Arthur J. Hopkins. We're all friends here though. You can call me Art."

* * *

I'd got stuck in traffic. Without the benefit of blue lights and sirens, I'd been forced to crawl out of the city. Once I reached the motorway, I'd put my foot down. Arriving at the house I found half a dozen police cars outside, blue lights flashing, doors agape. With the adrenaline surging like never before, I slammed on the brakes and was almost out of the car before it had fully come to a halt. I saw that the place was full of people. Officers, journalists. I locked eyes with Alex, and had the compulsion to smash him in the teeth for betraying me. It was then, as I pushed my way in, that I saw him.

Benton.

He was handcuffed already, but seemed unconcerned. A tray of spilled champagne was at his feet, but that didn't matter, it might as well have been just him and me in the room. He shifted his eyes to the sheet-draped mass beside him. Just by the smell I knew what was under there, even without whatever had spilled out of it. He was watching me stare at it, and I nodded to one of the officers to remove the sheet. He did as he was told, and the room collectively gasped as one. All but me and Benton, that is. I locked eyes with him, and he with me. I could see well enough what he had displayed in my peripheral vision, but I was determined not to show him that he had repulsed me. The cold dead woman with 'press here' etched into her stomach. I could hear people in the background. Some vomiting, others were taking pictures. I only stared at Benton, and for the first time wondered which of us was the bigger monster. I don't know where it came from or why I did it, but I looked him in the eye... and smiled.

"This is it? This is the big plan to shock?" I said to him. "You failed. You got caught. I'm going to see you rot in prison. Six months from now, nobody will even remember your name."

The constant click of the cameras and the strobe effect of the flash was driving me insane, and I spun around and glared at the poor officer.

"Get these wankers out of here! Confiscate the cameras. This is a fucking crime scene!"

The officers stopped gawping and snapped to attention. I would like to think it was because I was the ranking officer, but I think it was more likely because I was still wearing that crazy smile. I turned back to Benton, who was still watching me, a semi amused smirk on his lips. I walked towards him standing less than a foot away before one of the officers stopped me from getting any closer.

"Was it worth it? Was it worth ruining your life for this?" I asked, my voice taking on a shrill tone. I was angry, elated, confused, and just a little bit afraid.

He stared at me, and with just one gesture, despite the fact that he was in cuffs and surrounded by officers, he was in charge. He rolled his eyes to the ceiling, and then turned his gaze back at me with a mixture of arrogance and supreme confidence.

"Watch him," I said to one of the officers as I started to back away.

My heart thundered against my ribcage as I increased my speed, then started to jog towards the steps.

"Wait, sir, up there isn't secured," an officer said as I pushed past him, taking the steps two at a time. I threw open the first door, the stench coming from within only made more real by the steady drone of flies swarming around the mess on the bed. There was a girl, her empty eye sockets like twin pools of darkness in the gloom. She had been decimated, flesh peeled away, leaving only a pulpy mass of sinew and muscle that reminded me of those diagrams in doctors' offices showing the human anatomy.

The flesh that Benton had gone to such great pains to remove was still in the room though. It had been used as a blanket of sorts to cover her flayed corpse. As I looked closer at the putrid, blue grey mass covering her, I noticed there was more than should be there. It was hard to make out, difficult to mentally put together where everything should go. It was at that point that I noticed that there were actually two complete human skins draped over her, not sure where the second body is though. Angry flies buzzed past my face, and I swatted them away as I looked at the display he had left me. And that's exactly what it was. A display. A piece designed to shock. I could almost see the artistic merit of it. There was even a sign, penned in the same hand which had been on the packages he'd sent to me. It was written on white card on one of the display posts I recognised from the Art gallery. The son of a bitch had named his handiwork.

On a cold winter's day

I hated to admit it, but the name fit the piece perfectly. If shock was his intention, then shock was something he had certainly achieved. I knew there was more though. As disturbing as it was, this didn't feel like the grand finale Benton wanted. I looked at the door to my right, the only other one which was closed. Even before I saw Perkins standing outside it and the ghostly expression on his face, I think on some level I knew what was waiting for me.

"Martin, no…" was all he got to say before I shoved him aside and flung the door open.

It was like being hit in the face. Everything left me then, and I distinctly felt something switch off in my brain. I wanted to ask for help, for someone to do something, but by then I was already screaming.

THURSDAY

30.

I couldn't help laughing when I heard Detective Andrew's screaming. He gets it now. He understands where he fits in. The final piece. The human angle in my story; something the other pieces had lacked. To the world they were just more dead bodies to add to the ever growing pile of deceased men and women in this harsh world. Now, though, they have Detective Andrew's face to go with it. The broken man. The face that will be remembered by society for not only being the one who had failed to catch me but also the one who'd lost his own wife in his struggles. Not just his wife but also his colleague and friend - the man who tried so desperately hard to protect the wife from my advances despite being in no condition to offer a threat. The man who'd failed. I smiled again as I remembered the 'struggle' I'd had with Andrew's partner.

I knew going after the two of them was going to be a risk but I also knew it was one which was worth taking. Right there and then it could have been the end of the line when I'd made my first move. It would have been too had I not managed to completely catch them by surprise. The first blow to the back of the man's head was enough to knock him to the floor but not enough to knock him out. All because I'd mistimed the swing and hadn't connected as solidly as I'd hoped.

Of course, at the time I'd thought he was out for the count, so I'd turned my attention to the screaming wife. One of her hands was raised to protect her head from the possibility of having a brick swung at it, the other hand over the bump in her stomach. Ah, the bump. The joy I'd felt when I'd realised she was pregnant. Instantly I'd known the scene I was going to create from the two pieces of the puzzle. It was then I'd advanced towards her with a grin plastered across my face. I stopped short when I heard a groaning from behind. I turned on the spot, and was surprised (and impressed) to see the man standing. He swayed around as though dazed. His fists were clenched, ready for a fight. I'd chuckled and turned to the wife, telling her to wait right there.

The man hadn't stood a chance. He took a feeble swing which, of course, missed and I planted the brick firmly in his face. The crunch was satisfying, to say the least, as his nose crumpled to almost nothing. He dropped to the floor. He was unconscious this time round. Good thing too.

When I'd turned to the wife she was running. Why, I had no idea. She wouldn't be getting away. She wasn't going anywhere. Not in her state; the bump slowed her down. The bump. That lovely bump, and the possibilities which it opened up for me.

I'd chased her down with ease and knocked her to the floor before throttling her into a state of unconsciousness too - just as I'd done with the schoolgirl and the whore. The stirrings below, just like the ones I'd experienced before, were powerful and I desperately wanted to release myself there and then - give myself the climax my body was calling for. I didn't though. I couldn't. I didn't want to waste it. Not when there was a bump to play with. Not when... the baby.

I knew there had been a blackness in me. Before the sexual urges, before the killing. It was only when I reached up, fully lubed, with the razor sharp knife into Mrs Andrew's bloody vagina and cut the baby awkwardly from within, accidentally slicing it here and there while doing so, that I realised how dark the blackness really was. For this, someone would need to invent a darker colour to have described the state of my soul.

Of course I hadn't cut the baby out where I'd knocked the man and the wife out. I'd managed to get them into the van. Sure I wanted to kill them immediately but I couldn't. I just knew that Detective Andrews would have been expecting a phone call to be made. It was clear, from the bags the wife had left the house with, that he was sending her away with an officer for protection so I thought I'd play safe and get them both to make a call to him when they regained consciousness - cuffed together in the upstairs bedroom.

Just thinking about getting them up those stairs made me start to sweat again. That had been a heavy night...

Of course neither of them had wanted to make the call. They needed encouragement. A knife to her throat and a knife to his. When she made her call, I slid the blade across the man's throat, slicing through his windpipe and arteries. He bled out quickly with a satisfying, bubbling spray. At the time I was surprised at my lack of sexual urges as I watched the life gush out of him. I was almost disappointed, at least I *was* almost disappointed... When I then crushed the life from Mrs Andrews and my thoughts moved back to the tiny life, fading within her cooling corpse, the urges had returned. With a vengeance.

I couldn't help laughing again as I sat in the back of the police car. The officer in front turned to face me and asked what I was laughing at but I didn't answer him. He hadn't been upstairs yet. He hadn't seen what I'd done. He was merely babysitting me. He'd hear soon enough, though. The whole world would.

"Freak..." the officer said as he continued to stare at me. I didn't verbally retort. There was no need. I merely gave him a friendly wink. He should be thanking his lucky stars. He has no idea who he is sitting in the car with. He has no idea just how well known I am going to be. If he did - he wouldn't be name-calling. He'd be begging for my autograph. Of course - he'd have to take the cuffs off first. But if he did... I'm pretty sure I'd have to take care of the stirrings below as I remember what I did to mother and child.

I laughed again.

* * *

My wife was sitting in a chair, our unborn baby, no more than a slick, bloody mound clutched in her arms. Wyatt was propped up behind the chair, dead hands clasped on her shoulders, his bruised head lolling on his chest due to the knife wound which had slit his throat almost to the spine. I screamed again, my pained cry reverberating around the room: I couldn't help but stare at what he'd done, at the level of depravity that he had gone to. There were... things protruding from what remained of my unborn child, things placed in its undeveloped body by Benton. Like a passenger in my own body, I staggered into the room, pushing Wyatt's corpse aside, ignoring its dead man's stare as his head lolled and his body crumpled to the floor. I took Lucy's face in my shaking hands and put my head to hers. I knew she was gone, it was plain just by looking. I willed her to live anyway, but her skin was cold, and her body already starting to putrefy.

"Come back to me," I screamed, cupping her hands in mine, tears and snot running down my face. I didn't care, I had already lost everything.

"Just come back to me," I repeated, looking into her dead, doll-like eyes and praying for some flicker of recognition.

I vaguely heard Patterson in the distance, telling people to get me out of the room. I turned and screamed at them not to touch me, My eyes blurred with tears. They backed off and I turned back to Lucy. Her lower half was a fleshy mess where Benton had cut the baby out of her. I glanced down at it, hoping against hope that there would be nothing there human I would recognise, but the tiny, perfectly formed hand burned into my brain, and that miniature, screwed up face was something that would haunt my every waking moment until the day I died.

I grasped Lucy's face again and put my hot forehead against her cold one. It came to me then. The message she had left me on Saturday night. I thought it was just a check in, and that she was perhaps upset about having to leave, but now, in context, it made sense.

Benton had made her call. Benton had made her say her goodbyes just as he'd made Wyatt call me too. I glanced at Wyatt on the floor, at his bruised and beaten face. There was a distinct footprint, the tell-tale pattern of a boot across the side of his face. How he must have suffered and resisted before Benton had finished him off. It all fitted. It all made sense. With a shaking hand, I fished my phone out of my pocket and pressed the voicemail key, somehow remembering to set the phone to loudspeaker. I lifted Lucy's head and looked into her eyes as the message filled the room.

It's just me checking in… I don't know how this will all end… but I just wanted to tell you that everything will be alright, and that I love you no matter what…

The line had clicked off then, and I knew she had known she was about to die. Another scream welled up in me and was unleashed with such fury that I tasted blood in my throat.

I

Love

You.

Just three little words. Surely now I would be able to say them, surely now, in death was my one chance to put it right, to tell her how I felt. I wanted to, I wanted to more than anything I've ever wanted before. The words just wouldn't come. I blinked through tears at the distorted corpses of my family, and waited for those words to arrive. Instead it was another roar, a grunt. I knew then it was too late. Those words were never going to come. I was never going to be able to say them. As strong hands started to drag me away, I could only stare at her, my Lucy, my world. Why couldn't I say it? Why couldn't I let those words out? I wondered if I would wake in the night screaming them later, alone in a house as empty and dead inside as I was. It was possible, if I ever slept again, anyway. The will to fight was long gone along with my ability to stand, I let them drag me out of the room. I held on to the pain, held onto it like a security blanket.

Did I deserve it? Had the years as a liar and an insecure prick who was disillusioned with life made me worthy of such punishment? Or was I a victim? Another statistic, just a number to crunch in the database. A case file which would eventually be filed away, never to be seen again? Probably. Not that I cared right then. All I could think about was the pain, and how much I deserved to be feeling it.

I clutched the phone to my chest and replayed the message as they dragged me to the hallway. I listened to her words, the impact of what they'd meant hitting me harder and harder with each listen. I couldn't help myself. I played it again. Then again, and again, all the time with those images in my head as concerned officers buzzed around me. It was after that fifth listen when everything fell into place. Everything made sense. I looked back into the room, my training forcing me to look past the blood. It was then that I understood my part in the process. The signpost glimmering in the gloom, the scrawled hand perfectly readable from where I knelt in the hall.

Happy Ever After

I was half-led, half-dragged downstairs, but that didn't matter. What I'd seen would stay with me forever. The fleshy remains of the fat woman made sense now, and I knew what the purpose of the thing grafted into her stomach was.

"Press it," I screamed at Perkins who was standing beside the body, my throat raw and sore.

He glanced at Patterson, who then looked at me.

"I said press it!" I screamed again as I shook myself free of the officers who had dragged me from the room. Perkins hesitated, and then did as he was instructed. Music began to filter out of the putrid remains, and it all made perfect sense. I fell to my knees by the door and for some reason that I can't explain, I started to laugh. This was his way of telling me it was over. This was his way of letting me know it was done.

The fat lady was singing.

No wall mounted sign needed. Message received loud and clear.

I glanced outside to the patrol car containing Benton, and could see him watching me, a small smile on his face. My fellow officers were watching me too. A look of pity on their pale faces. It wasn't until then that I truly understood.

I was Benton's final piece. I was the grand finale. I was his masterpiece. He had won.

EPILOGUE

I bounced around on the hard back-seat as the van violently turned one of the last corners in our long journey. A little warning would have been nice. I heard the driver mutter something about there being a media circus ahead. His passenger uttered a swear word in response. From where I was sitting I couldn't see much despite my best attempts. A slight ache of disappointment as I felt as though I were being cheated from what I was owed.

Further conversation from the front of the van ended with the passenger getting on his radio to state we'd be going in via the back entrance. Further disappointment on my part as the van raced towards the end of the road.

The crowd they were talking about must have been big as - for a split second - I heard them shouting as we drove by.

All of them calling my name.

My real name.

Arthur J. Hopkins or variants of it at least.

My favourite being 'Art'.

I couldn't help but smile.

My only two regrets being that Detective Andrews wasn't sitting here with me to see that I was right - I would be known - and that the van hadn't stopped to let me see the faces in the crowds.

The disappointment was short-lived though as we turned another couple of corners - and the van began to slow - I heard more shouting and yelling. My name amongst the many words being screamed from the people waiting to see me. Of course there were negative words being thrown around too but I didn't mind. Art is subjective and it's nearly impossible to please everyone no matter how hard you try.

The van juddered to a stop as the shouting outside continued. I stood up and awkwardly straightened my suit jacket and tie. Would have been easier had it not been for the cuffs binding my wrists. A few seconds later and the back doors of the white transit van opened and I was finally confronted by a large crowd of people all surging forward to see me. Some had papers in their hands, some had signs, but mostly they had cameras - just as they had done in the dream I had back in my apartment when I started down this journey.

I laughed as I gave them all a wave and thanked them for coming to see me.

One of the officers helped me step down from the van as the other kept the crowd from getting close - helped by officers who had appeared from the courthouse.

I didn't get much of an opportunity to speak to my fans, and critics, as I was pushed towards the back entrance of the court. It didn't matter though. I didn't need to talk to them. I didn't need to engage in conversation as to whether they liked or disliked my work. Seeing them was enough. Knowing these people had come out to see me – that was enough. For as long as I live, I'll never forget this moment and the chants of the crowd.

If only mum and dad were here to see me.

Not a failure now, am I?

We walked through the doors of the courthouse and they slammed shut behind me, cutting the noise of the people outside short. Goodbye my friends. Don't forget me. Not that you'll be able to.

~ FIN

ABOUT THE AUTHORS

Michael Bray is a UK based horror author, hailing from Leeds, England. His debut novel, Whisper, went on to become a critically acclaimed best seller.

Influenced from an early age by the suspense horror of authors such as Stephen King, Brian Lumley and James Herbert as well as TV shows like Tales From The Crypt, The Outer Limits & The Twilight Zone, he spends his days muttering to himself at his computer and writing for his rapidly growing fan base.

WWW.MICHAELBRAYAUTHOR.COM

MATT SHAW was born, quite by accident (his mother tripped, he shot out) September 30th 1980 in Winchester hospital where he was immediately placed on the baby ward and EBay. Some twelve years later (wandering the corridors of the hospital and playing with road kill when he was on day release), the listing closed and he remained unsold, he was booted out of the hospital to start his life as a writer and hobbit - beginning with writing screenplays and short stories for his own amusement before finally getting published when he was twenty-seven years and forty-five seconds old.

http://www.mattshawpublications.co.uk/

Made in the USA
Middletown, DE
14 July 2018